After the Wink
and other stories

by Carolyn Steele Agosta

Published by
Carolyn Steele Agosta
North Carolina
Visit my website at http://www.carolynagosta.com

The stories are in this collection are works of fiction for
the most part; some are creative non-fiction. No
reference to any real person should be inferred, you
never know when I'm just making it up.

Grateful acknowledgement is made to the magazines
that originally published these stories and a complete
list may be found in the appendix.

Agosta, Carolyn Steele, 1952 –
After the Wink, and other stories / by Carolyn Steele
Agosta, 1st ed.

Summary: A collection of 38 short stories, most of
them previously published 1999-2008.

Cover photos by Inga Ivanova (front) and HAYKIRDI (back) used with permission.

ISBN 978-0-9829561-2-0

Published in the USA.

Dedicated to my family – Matt, Joanna, David, Katie, Brandon, Becky & Danny

Table of Contents

After The Wink

IT STARTS OUT so harmlessly.

I don't really mean anything by it, I'm just in one of those moods. I mean, when you're 42 years old and have 3 kids and a husband and responsibilities, who figures on finding excitement, too? Other than bad excitement, like when you have to hit the brakes hard and all your blood vessels get a quick *yee-ha*.

It's true, I've been noticing men a lot lately. Their arms, particularly. Don't ask me why, but I've suddenly become fascinated with men's arms. Forearms, lightly furred, with those lines of tendons and the swell of muscle below the elbow that women just don't have. And men's hands, square and capable. I see them everywhere. In restaurants, at gas stations, in the middle of the aisle at the freakin' K-Mart, for god's sake. It's embarrassing to know I'm lusting in Lawn & Garden.

It's not just the young men either, mind you. I've been noticing older men, too. Men in their 40's and 50's, men who maybe think no woman is looking at them that way anymore. Mostly I like the ones who still have plenty of hair and rugged looking faces, who look like they still get some, you know? Ponytails too, on older men, catch my attention. Here's a guy who thinks young, I figure. I could be wrong. Maybe he's just a guy who hates going to the barber.

Anyway, I'm sitting there at the coffee shop, I'm reading a book by Robin Hemley and it makes me laugh out loud. I look around to see if anyone notices and there's a man smiling at me. He's good-looking too. He's sitting at one of the tables, reading a magazine, and it's not just any magazine, not about motorcycles or computers or entertainers, it's the *New Yorker*. The guy's literate, for crying in the sink.

I give him a little smile. Going back to my reading, I shift in my seat, cross my legs, straighten my back a little. *Knockers up*, my aunt used to say. I rest my chin on my hand, arching my neck a little. That's body language for "I'm interested". Or something like that. A customer near the front makes a huge mess by dropping her coffee, the tray clattering to the floor. I take a quick glance at Mr. Attractive and he's looking at me. So I smile. And then, God help me, I wink.

Now it's just a little wink, just an acknowledgement that he's there and I'm there and we both see the humor of the situation and that, perhaps, we're somehow both a little more in the know than the average joker and already have this little connection, but that's all it is. I swear.

But it's enough.

Because next thing I know, he's picking up his coffee and his *New Yorker* and he's coming over to me, doing that little raised eyebrow thing to ask if he can join me and I'm nodding, nodding, thinking I don't quite believe this. He asks me about my book and I ask him about his magazine and I mention, modestly, that I'm a writer and he mentions, modestly, that he's a musician, and even though we're really a bookkeeper and a systems analyst, we understand that we're not defined by our paying jobs. I tell him my name and he tells me his and it's one of those names I always admired. He has a little bit of curly black/grey/white hair coming out of the collar of his shirt. His eyes crinkle at the corners and his forearms flex as he leans forward on his elbows to talk to me in low tones that require that I lean forward too. I smile to show my dimples and hope that I don't have coffee breath and we keep talking. About books and music and the theatre. About the way that parking is getting impossible in this town and how traffic is ridiculous. He mentions that he lives near South Park and I mention that I'm over by the university and pretty soon our coffee is cold and it's somehow gotten to be an hour later.

It's really time for me to leave and he walks me to my car, which thank heavens is decently clean, with no McDonald's Happy Meal figures on the front seat. He

3

mentions that he's going to the poetry slam next Friday because his friend is playing flute for some poet and I mention that I've never been to a poetry slam and he says I should try it. So I say maybe I will and I drive away with my hands perspiring on the steering wheel.

I have no complaints about my husband, that has to be understood. He's loving and thoughtful and sexy and he picks up his socks and puts down the toilet seat. But on Friday night I'm at the damn poetry slam, trying to look like I'm enjoying it but really keeping an eye out for Mr. Handsome only I don't see him and feel like a fool and I'm just getting ready to leave (I mean it, I'm only giving it five more minutes) when he walks in. And he winks at me.

The place is crowded and noisy, people are talking to each other and completely ignoring the woman in purple tights and purple hair who is bellowing some poem about spaghetti, and when he takes my elbow and leads me away to a quieter corner, a little thrill runs right up my arm. He asks if I want to get out of there and I nod and suddenly my knees are way too loose and I'm afraid that if I walk, they'll bend backwards, the wrong way, which would not be attractive at all.

I manage to pull myself together and we get in our cars and I follow him to a bar, which is quiet and low-lit and has a nice band playing oldies. We talk and dance and his arms go around my waist, which has mostly been used to apron strings and babies' monkey legs and my husband's arms. Which are also nicely hairy and brown and have those good flexy muscles. Which I'm trying not to think about just like I'm trying not to mention that both Mr. Gorgeous and I are wearing wedding rings. Because we are, and we're not kidding ourselves that this is anything but an exercise in visibility.

You see, it seems to me that after 40, you become invisible. Oh, you're still there and people see you but they don't really SEE you. They see this person whose daughter is now an adult and whose mother is now a child and who's supposed to hold everything together. A person who couldn't possibly have desires and doubts and unfulfilled longings. A person who is still, improbably, perhaps imperceptibly, a person.

I take a good look at Mr. Still-Has-It and I can see that he still loves rock'n'roll and still would look good behind the wheel of a Corvette and still has a bit of anxiety about how he looks to a younger woman. Which I am, to him. So I smile and flirt and he flirts back and it feel real good. We dance and I think about how strange it is to be in the arms of someone else, another man, a man who is a bit taller and bulkier than my husband, with a different voice and different lips and different eyes. It feels so weird, and then it feels even weirder when he kisses me, which he does, right there in the middle of the dance floor. I haven't kissed another man on the lips in over 20 years and now his mouth is on mine, and it's different, a different touch and taste and style. More than that, it's real, I'm really here and I'm doing this thing.

I start to shake, start to vibrate like a goddamn tuning fork, until he probably thinks he's such a good kisser that I'm going into orgasm, but actually I'm about three counties away from an orgasm. I'm just shaking with fear because I realize that I'm thinking about a lot more than kissing and that scares the hell out of me.

He laughs a little, softly, in a pleased sort of way, and I blush all the way to my fingernails and we go back to the table. He's looking at me and I think, *yes, look at me*. I'm not ready to be old, to have all my fun behind me. I want to shimmy when I dance, and wiggle when I walk. I want a man to look at me and get a little *yee-ha* of his own.

Then I begin to think that maybe this is why people cheat in the first place. To have this warm glow that comes from someone else's eyes. To remember who they are and not to be the person that everyone thinks they are and, a little bit, not to be the person they know they are.

I look at him too. I see a man who's just as scared as I am of becoming invisible. Or being seen as past it, on the far side of manhood, as being old. So I reach across the table and take his hand (good hands, wide and blunt-fingered, the hands of a man who can fix things). I stroke his wrist and tell him without saying it that he's still pretty sexy-looking and makes my mouth water. I think about all the things I've never done and all the things I'll never be, and I wonder if it's too late.

A rush goes through me, starting with my lips, making them feel warm and full, and I think, damn, what a hell of a time for my first hot flash. But it's not a hot flash. It's the realization that I'm not going to do a thing. Because among all those things I wanted to do with my life, this wasn't on the list.

I give Mr. It-Might-Have-Been a quick kiss on the cheek. I'll have daydreams for a while about him, play with thoughts that should send me to confession, and keep the memory of his kiss for those days when I can't jump-start my own desires. I drive home and sit for a moment in the car, looking up at the light in the bedroom window.

You know, sometimes a wink is really just a nervous tic, a sudden twitch of muscles contracted in error by a misguided neuron, an accident of synapses gone awry. The muscles keep twitching until something clicks over and they smooth out, like a skip in an old 45 rpm record, and everything goes back to normal. The way it should be, I guess. The way it is. The way the music plays best.

Jim

HE'S DEAD. JIM is dead.

I sit at the kitchen table. My coffee steams gently in its cup, music plays on the radio and next to me, the dog lies snoring. My life is unchanged. And yet. . . He's dead. Jim is *dead*.

The obituary in the paper doesn't tell much. "Lt. James Mays, 59, of Seattle, Washington, died November 7th at Veteran's Hospital. A 1969 graduate of Bingham High School and a U.S. Marine, he was awarded the Bronze Star for Bravery in Action in Viet Nam, 1972. He is survived by his mother, Mrs. Beverly Mays, of Bingham."

It doesn't mention family. No wife, no kids. I stare at the newpaper and think, surely this is a mistake. It must all be a mistake, he can't be dead, he can't have been 59, I can't be sitting here reading this. I turn the pages, fold the newspaper and reopen it, starting fresh. But it's still there and he's dead and I wonder whether it makes a difference.

He was always getting in trouble. Maybe that's why I was drawn to him—all good girls secretly wonder about bad boys. He was our token hippie, with his long hair and fatigue jacket, covered with peace symbols. At assembly, he refused to say the Pledge of Allegiance. Just couldn't pledge allegiance when the leaders of the country were so screwed up, he insisted. Only he didn't say "screwed" and he got sent to Detention. People noticed things like that in 1969.

Jim wanted to change the world. He took it all to heart—the black power salute at the Mexico Olympics, Nixon's election, the starving Biafrans. He was tall and good-looking in a rebellious sort of way and he could make dissention look attractive and fun. We painted posters and marched in protests and kissed in his beat-up old Falcon.

The day after they had the first lottery for military service, Jim came into the classroom looking green. His birth date had been pulled as the seventh position on the list. If he'd been born just 23 minutes later, he would have been number 307 instead. I didn't know then that Life turns on just such tiny moments. Events swing on a pivot, hold their course a breathless second, and then plummet in a new direction, taking us on a ride into an unalterable arc of centrifugal motion.

He loved me, he said. We were going to spend our lives together. I was 16. I understood nothing, practically nothing. He was facing the draft, military training, Viet Nam, and a quick, muddy jeep ride into desperation. I was choosing a prom dress.

Things were different then. People protected their children from the harsh realities of life. I lived in a Doris Day world where young men were handsome and alive, and girls were virgins until they married. "I could be dead by this time next year," Jim would say to me when I told him no. I'd cover my ears, I didn't want to think about it. He began running wild, drinking, doing drugs, skipping school. Someone said he was trying to sow all his wild oats before it was too late. I couldn't understand and I hated the drugs. He was going somewhere without me.

He asked someone else to the prom, Barb Kennedy. I knew why, we all knew why. Barb Kennedy put out.

A week after the prom, he came over. "Please go out with me," he said, and held out his hand. Our break-up was a bad dream, I thought. He still loves me. When we got to his car, I was disappointed to see that he had a friend along, Dave Markowski. I didn't care for him much; he was a big guy, a wrestler, crude and distasteful. We went to a basketball game but left before it was over. Both boys were high on something. They kept laughing over nothing and their eyes gleamed with danger.

Jim drove to a deserted road, pulled the car onto the shoulder, and turned off the engine. When he started to kiss me, I protested. "This is stupid, take Dave home," I said. "What do you expect him to do?" Jim looked past me to Dave and grinned.

"You're right," he said, not looking at me. "It's not really fair to ol' Dave." He smiled past me again and I heard Dave laugh. "Why don't we just share?" Jim looked at me and gave a sort of half-laugh, half-grunt.

I felt Dave's arms come around my waist from behind. "I've got a few ideas of my own, too," he said, his breath in my ear, his horrid wet lips on my neck. I stared at Jim in shock. He sat smiling, peaceful. Then he was on top of me, pressing me down, pressing me down. His mouth was on mine, wet and scraping, his lips that always before had been gentle. My blouse was ripped open; I bit someone and tasted blood. I felt hands, fingers, along my thighs, under my skirt, between my legs. I bucked and kicked, struggling to get free, hampered by Jim's weight, Dave's thick, ugly fingers around my wrists. "Pull her into the back," I heard Dave say and he climbed over the seat. My mouth momentarily free, I screamed, shrilly and hysterically. Jim stopped then, his face going white. I pushed hard with my feet, found the door latch and plunged out of the car. Then I was rolling, onto my feet, running across the field. Cold, wet weeds tore at my legs, I could hear my ragged breath and my pounding

11

heart. My knees gave way and I crawled, panting, to cling to a tree trunk. Pressing my face against the rough bark, I prayed that they weren't still out there, looking for me.

At the memories of that night, I suddenly have to stand, draw deep breaths and look out the window at the bright line of daffodils near the garage. Over forty years have passed since that night and I can still remember it all.

I never told anyone what happened. How I hid in the skeleton of an unfinished apartment building, smelling the raw lumber, watching for headlights. How I saw Jim's car come creeping along, the windows down, his voice calling my name.

I never told my mother, even though she heard me come in and tapped at the bathroom door to ask if I'd had a good time. Fine, I told her, great game. I scrubbed my skin raw with the rough side of the washcloth and eventually my legs stopped shaking.

I never told. How could I? It was too ugly, too cruel to put into words. The quick flashes of memory were bad enough—Dave's tongue slithering down my neck, blue-jeaned legs scraping against my thighs, the way Jim looked like a vaguely familiar stranger.

The next day my parents went out and Jim came over. He banged on the front door that I refused to open. He called through the window. "I'm sorry, I'm so sorry! I have to talk to you!"

"Go AWAY!" I screamed. "I hate you! Go away and leave me alone."

He was crying, I could see him. I love you, his mouth said, I'm so sorry. There was no sound, just the shapes of the words.

I didn't cry. I didn't feel sorry for him, I didn't feel anything. I turned and walked away.

I still had to go to class every day. Still had to see Jim in the halls and in History class. His eyes were cold and dead. I passed Dave in the hall, standing and laughing with his stupid friends. He called my name once, and I barely made it to the Girls' Room before I threw up.

The school year finally ended. Jim and Dave graduated, Jim left town. I didn't date again for a long time.

The next time I saw him, it was a year later. I had stayed after school to work on a Home Ec project. He was alone in the hall, wearing a Marine's dress blues. He stood straight and tall, proud, but his eyes looked old. "How have you been?" he asked quietly. How did he end up a Marine, I wondered. What kind of cataclysmic change had caused this? I wanted to hit him.

"Well, I see they've bought you," I said. He looked down at me, his eyes hooded. I barely heard his quick intake of breath before I pushed on. "I guess you're the Rebel who lost his Cause." Quickly, I walked away. At the end of the hall, I looked back. I could see him, outlined against the bright sunlight of the window. I couldn't tell if he was looking toward me or not. It didn't matter. I turned the corner and walked away.

I graduated from high school, started classes at U of M. The Beatles broke up, astronauts rode a dune buggy on the moon, we all stopped being kids. Eventually, the war ended. Women's Lib and Watergate took over the news. I met a man who kissed away my pain, we married, had children, made a good life.

And now he's dead. Jim is dead. And yes, it makes a difference. I'll never know whether he had regrets, as I did. He'll never know that I've wondered about him, tried to understand. That I've asked myself what would have happened if I'd given him one moment's grace the day he came back, the day I saw so much grief in his eyes. Life has a way of changing you, forcing you to stand in someone else's shoes. I learned that when my husband died, when a moment's inattention at the wheel took his life, took it suddenly and in a way that made me finally understand what it means to have the earth go unsteady under your feet. I knew what it was like to believe that all the rules have changed, and how it felt to want to hurt the only ones who love you.

If I thought of Jim at all, it was as that 18-year-old guy who broke my heart and taught me about love and betrayal. It seemed impossible to imagine him getting older, changing, becoming perhaps quite ordinary. For me, he would always be frozen in time, a young man coming of age in a frightening era of change. I often thought that Vietnam ruined him before he even got there. Perhaps it redeemed him, as well.

Me and Mom and the Very Bad Day

5:45   I hit the snooze button too many times, oversleep. Take stress reduction pill.

6:00   Older daughter oversleeps, blames me.

6:15   Younger daughter oversleeps, blames me. Son, however, wakes up bright and chipper.

7:15   Kids miss buses, have to drive them to three different schools. Younger daughter's school is 20 miles away.

9:15   Late leaving house for Mom's.

9:45   Get to Mom's, she's asleep and groggy. She apologizes.

10:00 We both go potty, leave for doctor's office, running late. Mom tells me saga of argument between

16

herself, my sister and their friend. Asks me to intercede.
I decline.

10:20   Mom has to go potty again, stop at Burger King
to do so. She apologizes.

10:55   Traffic heavy. Mom has to go potty again, has
been crossing her legs for 10 minutes already, no place
to stop. Finally find a Taco Bell.

11:00   Mom goes potty a little too late, has to change
clothes. She apologizes. I tell her to stop apologizing,
it's not her fault. I plan impassioned plea to doctor re
lighter dosage on diuretic.

11:15   Get to doctors' office. No handicap parking
available, sidewalk covered in ice. Slip-slide all the
way. They have no appointment for her. Turns out
doctor doesn't even work there anymore. They give us
new address. Leave, making way along sidewalk
covered in ice. Slip-slide all the way. Mom apologizes.

11:30   Finally find new office, after having to make
two U-turns. Mom apologizes. I say please stop
apologizing for what's not your fault. Crab at
receptionist re no notice of change of address.

11:45   Mom goes potty. Get shown into examining
room. Wait for doctor. Wait for doctor. Wait for doctor.
Mom asleep, nearly falls off table. She apologizes. I say
PLEASE stop apologizing for what's not your fault.
Feel like Scrooge chasing off carol-singing boys.

12:45   Ask them how much longer it will be. Explain Mom is diabetic, needs her lunch. One nurse asks another, who asks another, who asks another, who asks the doctor. He tells them an hour. Until she can get the echocardiogram, and then will still need exam and office discussion. I go AN HOUR!!!!!, doctor comes out of his office, explains he had   two emergencies, and says patients with chest pains come first (huffily). I say, sure they do, but couldn't somebody come let us know? We could have gone out and had lunch and come back. Mom says let's not wait. We leave. (huffily)

1:00   We go to McDonalds'. They screw up our order. Mom tells me of argument between herself, cafeteria worker at retirement home, and dining room partners. Asks me to intercede. I decline. Mom goes potty. I take additional stress reduction pill.

1:30   We leave McDonalds', head home. Mom quite cheerful, wants to go shopping for birthday cards. I say no, feel like Grinch stealing Cindy Lou Who's Christmas. I say, remind me to stop at post office. Mom spends rest of trip trying to put on gloves and failing to find thumb opening, nods off to sleep every few minutes.

2:15   Forget to stop at post office. Mom apologizes. I shout PLEASE DON"T APOLOGIZE. Feel like Mommy Dearest screaming about no wire clothes hangers.

2:30   Take mom home, explain to nurse at retirement center about no echocardiogram, no checkup, no impassioned plea.

2:45   While driving home, get speeding ticket for doing 70 in a 55 zone. Mumble to cop that I've had a bad day. He replies, it's not getting better.

3:00   Forget to stop at post office.

4:00   Go back to post office. Find card from doctor advising of move to new offices. Well, shit.

5:00   Husband calls home, gets tale of woe, takes me out to dinner. He's a keeper.

7:00   15-year-old daughter who has just finished classroom part of driver's training tells all her friends about my speeding ticket.

8:00   Mom calls to see if I've calmed down. Hears about my ticket from ever-obliging daughter. Mom apologizes. Tells me about new argument between herself, my aunt, and my cousin. Asks me to intercede. I decline.

9:00   Flush stress-reduction pills down toilet and just bang my head against the wall until I pass out. Ah, much better.

Just Hear Those
Sleighbells Jing-a-Ling

THE CHRISTMAS PARADE WAS LATER than usual that year, which meant that the mild North Carolina temperatures had given way to cold winds and overcast skies. Jane Creagan was one of the first spectators to arrive, coming directly from the high school where she helped suit up the seventy-two members of the Marching Spartans band. She had her two younger children, Dodd and Lisa, in tow and her husband, Gary, would meet them in front of Marzella's Nails & Tanning. Dodd was already jumping up and down, watching for the guy who always sold cotton candy and chocolate Santas. Lisa stood still and quiet, watching the crowd, ready to point out any iniquities. Sometimes Jane thought that Lisa was too sensitive for her own good; but then, she *was* fourteen years old, that terrible age when the truths of real life seep in.

"Look, Mom. That guy just pushed his way in front of that kid." Lisa nodded at a fellow across the street. "Just stepped right in front of him. That's not fair. That kid was there first."

"Never mind, Lisa. Let the child's mother sort it out."

"But she's not! She's just standing there, telling her kid to be polite. Don't you see? And nobody's telling that guy to be polite, and he's a grown-up, he should know better!" Lisa began chewing her upper lip, as she always did when distressed.

"Don't do that, you'll get all chapped. And mind your own business."

Jane checked her camera. She wanted to be sure to get photos of the band. It was Will's last year and she was so proud of him, becoming drum captain, getting accepted already at college. She didn't want to miss the opportunity to preserve the moment.

"How's it going?" Gary, her husband, came up behind her, hands in his pockets, breath already beginning to emit a little steam. The temperatures were certainly dropping now that the sun was going down. It was, after all, the shortest day of the year. The parade would be finishing up in near darkness.

"Mom! Mom! The cotton candy man!"

Dodd began jumping up and down so hard that Jane had to grab the back of his jacket to keep him from tumbling out in the street. The cotton candy man came toward them, smiling, dragging his wheeled cart full of sweets, toys, inflatable Rudolphs and novelty flashlights. Gary bought Dodd a violently blue cotton candy, shaking his head and saying, "If you throw up tonight, don't blame me." As the cotton candy man walked away, heading toward his next victim, Jane saw that his trousers were so low, the crack in his ass was showing. She turned to grin at Gary, who also saw and laughed.

"Oh my god!" Lisa grabbed her mother's arm. "Do you see that? He's mooning the whole crowd. Why doesn't somebody do something?"

"Yeah, you might be scarred for life." Gary put his arm around Lisa's shoulders. "Relax, honey. Don't make such a commotion. He's not doing it on purpose. Maybe he's poor and can't afford clothes that fit better. Maybe he lost his belt. Maybe…"

Lisa jerked away, frowning. "Stop it! You're making that up. He could pull his pants up if he wanted, but he doesn't want to. He *wants* to insult everyone here. He *likes* it. You know I'm right."

"Oh, jeez. Here we go again," Gary whispered to Jane.

Lisa heard him and turned her back, muttering, "Oh, I know. You guys think I'm over-reacting. Right. Like I'm over-reacting when I try to tell you about global warming. You'll be sorry when we all freeze to death, like in The Day After."

Jane sighed. They went through this all the time. It was getting a little old.

"Hey, that reminds me." Gary leaned closer, his lips at Jane's ear. "I had the weirdest dream last night. Remember that picture you showed me online, of Britney Spears? I had a dream that you did that – went out with no underwear, and flashed the paparazzi. Boy, that turned me on."

Jane laughed, almost choking, and turned to whisper back, "Oh great. That's a nice thing to talk about just before your son marches at his final Christmas parade."

"One thing has nothing to do with the other. I was just reminded of the dream by that guy's crack attack. So," he added, tucking his hands against her waist and pulling her up against him, "have you been a good little girl this year? Is Santa gonna give you the big one?" He pressed himself against her backside and despite her awareness of the crowd around them, Jane felt a little thrill run between her legs.

"Oh my *god*, do you have to do that in front of me?" Lisa stared at them, aghast. Her eyes were big and round, her face white, her voice unnecessarily loud. "Isn't it bad enough that I'm constantly exposed to assaults on my senses through the media? Do I have to witness it right in my own family?"

"For heaven's sake, Lisa, shut up!" Gary kept his voice low, but his message was clear. "No doom and gloom for one afternoon. Do you hear me? Be quiet!"

"Fine." Lisa turned her back on her parents, wiping her face on her sleeve. "The world could be ending and all you'd say is 'be quiet'. Look at the wind storms in Oregon this week. The snow in Colorado. Don't you people learn anything? The earth is spinning out of control. We're all going to die, and all you care about is Christmas shopping, and how much it's going to cost to send Will to college next year. Don't you realize? He's never going to make it. Our whole civilization will be collapsed by then."

Jane traded glances with Gary. Really, this whole thing was getting ridiculous. It was the damn school system. Every morning they made the kids listen to the news on classroom TV. No wonder Lisa was overwhelmed. A teenager had no sense of context, no realization that in every generation there was some big scare about the end of the world, and for what? The world was still ticking along, wasn't it?

The parade had started at last, along with a pattering of sleety rain. The JROTC kids marched down the highway with the United States and North Carolina flags. Jane took a couple of practice shots with the camera. The Red Hat Society ladies went by, dressed in their reds and purples. Brownies and Girl Scouts marched in straggling lines, the 4H club did a snappy rake-and-leaf-blower drill routine, and Jane got an excellent shot of a Civil War re-enactor in full uniform, shouldering his rifle and displaying a fearsome set of whiskers.

The sleet fell fast. People began to murmur and retreat further into their blankets, hoods and scarves. Jane made Dodd zip his jacket all the way up and put his gloves back on. His fingers were nearly scarlet with cold—combined with the blue stain, they looked purple. "You better watch out before they fall off," she teased him. Dodd just stared at her, snow beginning to catch on his eyelashes. "Dodd?" she asked. "Are you okay?"

"I can hear the band!" Gary leaned out over the road. "Yep, that's them. I see the flags of the color guard."

Lisa sat down on the curb, pulling her knees up and wrapping her arms around them. "I'm cold," she said. "It's really getting cold."

Jane checked her camera again. It was a digital, and fairly new, and she wasn't sure how good it was at action shots. She really wanted a good close-up of Will on drums. The sleet had definitely turned to snow. All around her, she could hear people talking about it. Snow! Yes, actual snow! They hardly ever got any. Maybe school would be closed tomorrow! A few of the kids tried to scrape together enough to make a snowball.

As the band drew nearer, Jane jostled for a good spot on the curb. Nobody was going to make her miss this shot. She felt, rather than saw, Dodd sit down on the curb to her left. "You're not going to be able to see anything," she warned, but he just leaned against her leg, huddled up in the cold.

It really *was* cold. She was having trouble holding the camera with her gloves on, so she took them off, shoving them in her pockets. Trouble was, the camera itself was so icy, she could barely stand to touch it. "Gary, we ought to have a fire in the woodstove tonight," she said. "In case the power goes out."

Now the first lines of the band were in view. Woodwinds—clarinets and flutes—followed by the saxophones. The drum line was always in the middle, so everyone would stay in beat. So many familiar faces passing her by—she knew all the kids by name—and each one concentrating on their playing, despite snow falling harder than ever, despite the flakes sticking to their lips and eyelashes. Jane kept the camera to her eye, even though her fingertips were frozen now, even though she had no feeling as far as her middle knuckle. She couldn't miss this shot. Lisa huddled against her right leg. Dodd against her left. "Turn me loose, guys, I'm about to fall over!" She laughed a little and glanced down at them. Before she could get more than a brief impression of two snow-covered mounds, she could hear the percussion section and looked up again, pressing the camera to her eye.

There was Will! He was beating away on the drums, his face set, intent on the cadence. His cap had fallen a little to one side, so that his dark hair was pushed up against the brim. She yelled, "You go, Will!", hoping to make him smile, but he remained at attention, staring straight ahead even when the tip of one drumstick snapped off in the middle of a beat. He just continued playing and marching, the red stripe on the side of his white trousers emphasizing the staccato regularity of his steps.

"They look fine. Don't they look fine?" she asked Gary over her shoulder. "Well, looks like Lisa was right about the storm. That ought to cheer her up for once."

Gary didn't answer. She turned to look and he was leaned against a lamppost, his eyes shut, his collar pulled up high. Snow lay almost in drifts on the folds of the muffler across his face. Jane started to put the camera back in her purse and two of her fingers broke off, snapping cleanly at the joint.

It was the damnedest thing. Didn't hurt. Not really, but how was she supposed to cook Christmas dinner with only eight fingers? Jane looked down again. Both the kids were buried under the snow already and most of the people around her were indistinct masses of white. "But this is crazy," she said. Half a block away, the band continued down the street to the strains of "Good King Wenceslaus", their red capes waving jauntily as one by one they began to fall over sideways, like slow-moving bowling pins. "It's crazy, isn't it? Gary?" He didn't answer. All around her, everything was covered in snow, and the parade had come to a complete halt. "This isn't right!" she cried out. "What's going on? This isn't how we do things around here!"

Oh, Natalie!

HIS VAN, RED AND WHITE, SIMILAR BUT not identical to an ambulance (Significant?), is parked in front of the gas station pump, while he, shabby and middle-aged, similar but not identical to Leon (Significant?) purchases one 16 ounce bottle of Coke and one package of Lance Nip-Chees.

The side door, unlocked, a swift sliding open and closed, back of the van filled with bins, locked (why?), smelling of gasoline and sugar, gag-me syrups, a duffle bag, sleeping bag, he is going further than just the next town. Surely, surely he will not begrudge me a few miles, a temporary shelter.

We are ten miles down the road before I show myself, before I come creeping out from behind the blue tarp, the 39-gallon Hefty Leaf & Lawn bag. His eyes, whites showing all around, his grasp on the wheel shattered as we sway from lane to lane. Does he think I'm going to hurt him?

(Note to self: Leon knew who she was before she asked for his help. Significant? Probably.)

29

No, he says. And no, and no again. He has a job to do; having me along will just complicate things. I point out the snow, drifting higher with each moment, I point out my flimsy jacket, my flip-flops. I mention my more-than-passing resemblance to Natalie Portman.

No.

Just for a while then, I ask, just until we reach Georgia. He won't get in trouble; I'm older than I look. (Many people have commented on my demeanor. I'm already grown up. From now on, I will just get older.)

He's had his fill of teen-aged girls, he says. He's had his fill of parades and people and cold. He likes the cold, but he's heading for warmth.

I could be his apprentice. I could learn to make cotton candy, to hawk his wares, to sell inflatable Rudolphs and Santas and giant candy canes. We could work the carnie circuit all the way to Florida. He could be my mentor, my salvation, my Leon. (Note to self: Of course, Leon dies at the end. Not so good for him.)

Get out of my van, he says. I'm not crossing the state line with any jailbait. Whatever you're running away from, it's not my problem. What did you do, fight with your folks?

I killed them, I say. And now I'm running from the law.

That's it, get out! He pulls off the road, stops his van in front of a church with a life-size Nativity scene set up in front of it (Significant? No room at the inn? Or in

30

the van?) He pushes me but I hang onto the seat with both hands. He gets out, comes around, slides open the door, I jump over into the driver's seat, put the van in gear, slam down the accelerator.

Oh, the surprise on his face. I have to laugh.

I drive the van around in a circle, spitting gravel from beneath the tires, stop in front of him. Hey, just kidding, I shout. I didn't kill them, I just talked back a little and they nearly died from shock. Get in. You can drive, but let's get moving. I was not elected to watch my people suffer and die while you discuss this invasion in a committee.

(Seriously, I don't think he even knows who Natalie Portman is. Has he never seen Star Wars Episode I? Or II, or III? What planet has this guy been living on?)

Look, mister, just until the state line. Please? (Meanwhile looking at my watch. He's making me lose a lot of time.) He starts driving again but I can see him giving little glances. I don't mind. Profile shots are my best.

So, why'd you shave your head, he asks after we pass through Columbia. Because, I say. Because there is something terribly wrong with this country, isn't there? Cruelty and injustice, intolerance and oppression. And where once you had the freedom to object, to think and speak as you saw fit, you now have censors and systems of surveillance coercing your conformity and soliciting your submission. How did this happen? Who's to blame?

Personally, I blame my parents.

He laughs. (Honestly, has this man never gone to the movies? Does he not own a DVD player?) He says, your parents are Republicans, right?

Why do you say that, I ask. (What does he know? Have I given myself away?)

Just a wild guess, he says, pulling out a cigarette. He lights it, lets the smoke out in a long sigh. (I roll down my window, despite the freezing cold. Does he think I want to get cancer? Some people are incredibly careless of other people's rights. And I do have rights, even if I'm only fifteen. Despite what my parents may think.) And besides, everyone says Natalie Portman really looked amazing with a shaved head. She has the kind of beauty that transcends fashion's dictates.

My eyeballs are beginning to hurt. (Neck, stiff. Shoulders, tense. Yes, probably another spell coming on. Signficant?) I try to breathe slow and deep, in through the nostrils, out through the mouth, but it only makes me take in massive amounts of tar, nicotine, and other carcinogens. But I am strong, no one can make me break. Natalie didn't break even when they were going to torture her. I can be like that. (Note to self: remember how she held her head high when they were going to march her behind the chemical sheds. Also when she realized the Republic had become corrupt.

32

After all, you can't blame Natalie for her lines. She didn't write them. I, at least, can still speak for myself.)

The van comes to a complete stop and it's not until then that I realize I've been sleeping. We're further south now, I can tell, the air is warmer, humid, the sun is much lower in the sky, the freaky snowstorm has faded away. The end of the trail, he says. Last rest area before the state line. You have to get out.

I ask if he'll consider driving across the state line, pulling over, and letting me walk across on my own and get back into his car, but he shakes his head. No beans.

Nothing can disappear. Nothing can ever not be, once it has been. He will be my Leon, even though he doesn't die but simply go away. Despite his incessant putrification of the air with cigarette smoke, and his saggy draggy jeans, he's been an alright guy. I tell him, Leon, I think I'm falling in love with you. It's the first time for me, you know?

He blinks. My name's not Leon. And you're one weird kid.

He drives away. I watch the taillights of his van (not really like an ambulance at all, more like a FedEx truck or UPS. Significant?) as they disappear into the night (not really night, more like late afternoon, but close enough). I'm alone once more. As she is usually alone. The outsider. Like in Closer (the movie, not the TV show), but without the pink hair. The rest area map shows me I am in Hardeeville, South Carolina, which is a pretty stupid name for a town, but it's the farthest I've made it yet. There are phones here. I could call my mother (the senator) and her husband (the psychiatrist). Tell them I'm out of meds and money. It wouldn't be the first time. Or the twenty-first. Or I could stay here and know, when I've strayed the most from their house, I've come the closest to home. (Note to self: find public library with internet, google 'patient's rights'. Can they *make* me take my meds? Am I legally insane if I don't want to? Also, check name of Natalie's agent. I used to know it.)(Also publicist.)

There are a lot of cars moving through this rest area. One truck, red with a camper back (Significant?) is parked at the dark end of the lot, while the guy getting out (tall, slender, cool suede jacket) smiles a little as he passes me. He has not bothered to lock the truck (Significant? I think yes.). He could be a Jedi, there is that something about his aura. And I have never been to Georgia.

Frozen in Place

NINE YEARS AFTER THE BIG STORM, Jivey Booth stopped by my bar and I just closed the place down right then and there, and spent the rest of the day with him, drinking coffee, smoking cigarettes. We talked about the storm, holed up as we'd been in a fleabag motel outside Durham, North Carolina, no heat, no light, no food, and about the things we'd done since then. He'd done a spell in jail, six months for stealing his girlfriend's ATM card, cleaning out her account. But when he considered how long a sentence he could have had, for many other things, he couldn't complain. I'd done a spell in the marriage cage but "Nothing that stuck," I told him. "Clean separation; no runs, no hits, no errors." At one point he mentioned Amy, his face reddening slightly. She was married now to some chiropractor in Charlotte. Coupla kids. He'd always felt bad about how things had gone down, but no point in going over all that again. Jivey ran his hand through

35

that bright gold hair, thinning now, and shot me one glance with his spooky blue eyes.

"I just didn't know," he said. "How was I to know?"

At that point, I poured the rest of the coffee down the sink and pulled out the Dewar's. Found us some peanuts behind the bar, turned on the CD player—some old Bob Segar stuff. "Shoot," I said, "remember the storm? Remember breaking into the vending machine? Living on Snickers bars and Fritos until they ran out and then wrapping ourselves up in those mangy old bedspreads and walking to the Bojangle's? Snow so high, I was tippy-toeing to keep my balls clear. We jimmied the lock on the back door and it just snapped, just plain shattered, remember?"

"I remember those damned frozen biscuits and sweet potato pies. Can't even look a sweet potato pie in the face any more."

It all came back. Playing poker and gin rummy until we were too cold to hold the cards, until our minds were numb. Swapping every story we ever knew, singing every drinking song we'd ever heard. Falling asleep in that weird silence, light filtering through the window shades odd and white because of the moon on the snow. Waking up disoriented, not knowing the time of day, or day of the week.

"Remember Grover?" he asked.

Hell, yes. The old guy in his car, frozen to death. Mouth hanging open, skin all blue. We named him

Grover, just so we could laugh about it and not freak out. Every couple of days we'd wrap up and go out in the cold, trying to see if anyone else was alive. Grover's was the only face we saw.

"Hell," I said, "we lived through that, we can live through anything. Nothing could be worse than those seventeen days, wondering if anyone had survived. And then trying to get things back to normal. But we survived, and so did a lot of other people and look at us now." I glanced around at my bar, at the business I'd built, the life I'd regained.

And Jivey nodded. "Yeah, and I'm not in jail," he laughed. "Who'da thunk?"

"So whatever happened with your dad?" I asked, what I'd wanted to ask all along. "He never brought you into the business?"

Jivey shrugged. "Nah. Probably just as well. I never could remember to wear my sunglasses and, with these eyes, somebody would have recognized me sooner or later. Dad and I don't talk any more. I phone Ma once in a while. She's the one who told me about Amy." He shifted in his seat, stubbed out his cigarette, laughed a little. "Last thing Dad ever said to me was when I tried to explain why I kept screwing up. Told Dad I had A.D.D. He just blew a gasket. 'A.D.D., my A.S.S. You're just plain stupid!' But I didn't care. After that last job, at Amy's folks' place, I had no heart any more for smash-and-grab. I always felt like it was my fault, you know? If I'd known it was her folks' shop, I never would've gone in there, never would've robbed them. Her dad wouldn't have run off crazy like that, her ma wouldn't have committed suicide. All those things, you know, all those things from one damned botched job, where all I got from the cash register was a lousy four hundred bucks anyway. A lousy four hundred bucks. Amy, dropping out of college. And out of my life, never knowing what a scumbag I am. Well, she's better off."

He sat there staring at the ash on his cigarette. "Doesn't matter," he finally said. "She's better off."

I got up then and cooked a couple of burgers on the grill. We talked about other things—football, his job as a truck driver traveling I-40, my plans to expand the bar. We washed the burgers down with more Dewar's, and I told him not to drive. He could sleep on the futon in the office. "It'll be like camping out," I said, "like holing up in that ratty motel in Durham."

Jivey shook his head and lit another one. "Not quite. Even in the middle of that damn storm, when there was nothing but white around and the air so cold you couldn't breathe, I really figured we'd come through it, ya know? Like there was a whole life ahead, something still to look forward to, a long road in front of me. Now I know the it's just a case of hit one end of the road and then turn around, head all the way back again. Just keep doing it every damn day until I die, just keep rolling.

Well, better than being frozen in place like old Grover, right?"

"Yeah," I said, watching his spooky blue eyes focus on something far away. "No Grovers around here."

Coming to My Senses

ONE MORNING I WOKE UP and smelled the coffee. This was strange, because I'd never been able to smell it before.

Phil paused in mid-whistle, snapping his newspaper shut and putting it in his briefcase. "No, the usual kind. Why?"

I stared down at the cup, huddled into my robe, my bare toes curling away from the cold floor. "I can smell," I said, wondering if I should add, "Eureka!"

"What do you mean?"

"I mean I can *smell!*"

I had always been clueless when it came to scents. There were very few odors I could detect at all, and the ones I did recognize, I got wrong. My family thought it was funny. If there was a messy job to do, one with unpleasant smells, a general cry would go up of "Get Diane to do it."

Now, however, I could smell things as they really were. I familiarized myself with all the scents that everyone else had taken for granted long ago. So *this* was "the musty odor of old books," and *that* was "lemon-fresh Pledge." I learned the oily funk of Grandpa's old player piano, and discovered why everyone else found chocolate so appealing. I knew when my daughter was menstruating and if my son had bothered to wash.

Phil was delighted. One night in bed, I stuck my nose into his armpit and those strong male pheromones filled me with such a rush of lust that I practically attacked him. After that little experience, he found ways to entice me with a variety of olfactory delights, from colognes to oils to good old-fashioned sweat. Our sex life underwent a serious upswing. In the mornings after he went to work and the children left for school, I curled up in the big bed and reveled in the fragrance of our lovemaking. Sometimes, in the midst of a PTA meeting or while driving the car, I would sniff the back of my hand, rub warm skin against my nose and breathe it in again, my own special scent, the essence of *Me*

It became an obsession, the discovery of new smells. I liked to go to the fruit market and the delicatessen, get drunk on blasts of grapefruit and kiwi, choose new ingredients like chicory or basil, prosciutto and chard.

My daughter fussed. "You didn't pick me up after school, I had to WALK home!" I'd been distracted at the garden center, choosing between jasmine and gardenias, sidetracked by fennel and spruce. "Aren't you ever going to be normal again?" she asked.   My son took to pinching my nostrils shut any time he wanted attention. "Sorry, Ma, you had that spaced-out look again, like you've been into the paint thinner. Not good." I received phone calls from my sisters. "We're worried about you," the eldest said. "You're not available any more to baby sit or run errands for Dad. What's gotten into you?"

Everything, I wanted to say. The trees and grass and the sweet smell of sun-dried hay. The metal tang of freshly turned earth. I woke each morning before the alarm rang, anxious to find what scents the day would bring. They were all so new. Sickly-sweet gasoline and eye-crossing gym socks. Funky little boys and babies' warm necks. Pizza. Tar. Fresh newspapers. Beer. But when I tried to explain, I only got, "But honey, everyone can smell. You'll get over it."

I didn't want to get over it. Even the "bad" odors didn't bother me, they were just as new and interesting as the "good" ones. Phil chased me all around the house one day with a sour dishcloth until we collapsed, laughing, on the couch. The children muttered in awkward dismay. Parents weren't supposed to laugh like that. It was gross.

I caught a cold and went into a panic, afraid my sense of smell would disappear forever. "I cad *stad* this," I said, blowing into a hanky. "I'b goig bad."

"Oh, lighten up," Phil said. "It's a cold, not the seven plagues of Egypt. Besides," he added, "even if you did lose your sense of smell again, you'd still be you. Things wouldn't change, would they?" He put his hands on my waist and pulled me close. "We're so good together now, nothing can ruin that, right? Right?"

The cold made me more determined not to waste a moment. I felt as though all of my senses had sharpened and I was bristling with antennae quivering with sensation. I loved it. I *loved* it. Through the internet, I found other enthusiasts and we messaged each other endlessly about herbal extracts, aromatic essences, lost recipes for historic perfumes. I collected samples—bergamot and vetiver, sandalwood and musk. In the grocery store, I followed a man for seven aisles, just because he smelled like new lumber.

"You spent all evening talking to that jerkface in the sweater," Phil complained after a party.

"It was his aftershave," I explained. "I couldn't quite isolate the components, but I'm sure it included cedarleaf and lime. Are you jealous?" I asked, suddenly pleased. "We only talked. I don't even remember his name."

"Yeah, well, I bet he'll remember yours." He stared at me, a faint line showing between his brows. "You don't want to get carried away with this, Diane," he said. "People are starting to talk."

My sisters convened and took me to dinner. "You're getting ridiculous," my elder sister said. "You were seen in the park, kneeling in the dirt with your face buried in some old lilac bushes. Are you crazy?"

I twirled the spaghetti strands on my fork. There was cinnamon in the sauce, and a touch of almond. "They were Agincourt Beauties," I said. "Don't you understand? If I'd gone from blind to seeing, you'd call it a miracle."

"That's different."

"Not to me." I set my fork down, and looked around the table at them. "I have lilacs in my life now! Honeysuckle! I never expected this, didn't even know what I'd been missing. I'm *happy,* for crying out loud."

She looked me over. "Maybe you need therapy."

"Yeah, aromatherapy," our younger sister giggled. "A twelve-step plan for the aromatically addicted. Back to normal by the end of the month."

"Sorry if I'm not doing this right," I said, pushing my plate away. "I didn't realize there was a timetable for joy."

Their disapproval clung like cheap perfume. Perhaps it was a shameful selfishness, this greed for sensation, this avarice for a significant fume. I dutifully visited my father in the nursing home, but even then I was collecting and storing impressions of the emanations of old age and the spoor of death. If I could think about odors at a time like that, maybe I *was* crazy—losing my mind instead of coming to my senses.

One evening, Phil watched me work in the garden. The back yard was fragrant with honey-melon sage and citrus southernwood, sylvetta and thyme.

"You look tired, hon," he said. "Why don't you relax?"

"I'm fine," I said, stooping to loosen the soil. "I wish people would stop fussing at me."

"Well, you seem uptight."

"Look, I was *great* until everyone else got all bent out of shape." I stood up and pressed the back of my gardening glove to my eyes. "Okay. Maybe I am a bit... frantic. What am I supposed to do with this gift? I've been given a whiff of fougere, but what good does it do me if I'm going to spend my life surrounded by Glade Extra-Fresh?"

"But hasn't it made your life richer?" he asked. "Isn't that really what the senses are for, to enhance your life, not drive it? When is it enough?"

"I don't know, but I feel passion about something for the first time in my life and I want to follow where it leads."

Phil looked at me for a long moment. "I thought you felt passion for me."

I didn't know what to say. I put my arms around his waist and held him close. "You know I do," I said, sniffing in his familiar scent, so warm, so comforting.

His skin, his shirt, his after-shave. And something else. I pressed my nose against his throat and tried again. Yes, I could smell it. The sulfuric reek of resentment.

In bed that night, lying beside him, trying to sleep, I became aware of the emotions seeping out his pores. The lemony scent of ambition. A spicy fume I identified as competitiveness. And beneath it all, almost masked by the redolence of male ego, the heart-aching current of loneliness. I wasn't sure I wanted that knowledge. Did perception require action? Phil's eyes were closed, and I couldn't help noticing how the little crinkles at the corners were deepening into furrows.

I curled up against him and he turned and took me in his arms. "I love you," I said.

"I know." He sighed and kissed my shoulder. "I know you do, honey. And I'm sorry to be a crank. When all this began, it was fun. I got a kick out of watching you run around like a kid on her first trip to Disneyland, but now..."

"Now?"

His voice was low. "Now, it feels like I'm competing with some other lover."

I could hardly breathe. The pain in his confession hurt me, but more than that, his breath exuded such envy and fear.

"I'm sorry," he said. "I want all of the good stuff and none of the bad, and I know that's unfair. But I can't help how I feel."

He rolled over and away from me. I pulled the sheet up to my face. Better to be suffocated by fabric softener and detergent than to deal with the vapor of guilt.

In the morning, I made coffee. Watching the steam rise, I told myself *no big deal.* It was just coffee, a dark-brown liquid, nothing more. Phil sat at the kitchen table, listening to the morning news. I had to turn my head away from the stench of self-reproach and insecurity that roiled in his stomach.

"I hate that this is coming between us," I said. "There's got to be a way to compromise."

"If you could just try to keep it under control," Phil said. "Not get so carried away."

"I need to change, you mean. Keep my dreams pocket-sized." There seemed nothing else to say so I began running water into the sink, adding soap, putting in dishes. The electric clock hummed on the wall and upstairs my son murmured in his sleep. Somewhere outside, a bird began his morning song. Maybe Phil was right, maybe they were all right and I was the foolish one, thinking I could ever be special. The bird's trill rose up a key and I thought, *but once you know, you can't not know.* How could I ever go back to that narrower life? I started scrubbing the dishes and listened as the bird, whatever it was, trilled through a half-dozen different songs. "Do you hear that? He's singing his little heart out. Brand new day, brand new start."

"What are you talking about?" Phil came over to me and put his hand on my shoulder.

"The bird. Don't you hear him? He's as loud as a whole flock."

"I don't hear anything," Phil said. "The window is closed. How can you hear him?" I became aware of the rustle of fabric as his fingers tightened on my sleeve. Far above us, an airplane droned in melodic counterpoint to the bird's song. Someone's radio played classical music. Tchaikovsky, Swan Lake. Oboes and bassoons traded places with flutes and violins. Funny how I'd never noticed before the whirring sound of bicycle tires from the kid delivering the newspaper, or the little rumble the kettle made before it whistled.

"I asked how you could hear that bird. Are you listening to me?" Phil's voice rose in an A-minor arpeggio. Outside, leaves rustled like taffeta and my heart lifted on the breeze that whispered softly as a lover in my ear. A tiny ripple of pleasure ran over me with each sigh of my pores breathing. "Diane? What are you listening to? Diane? *Diane?*"

48

...in Love and War

AS DAN DRIVES AWAY, I see a fresh bag of trash sitting on top of my garbage can. His. For a moment, I picture myself running after that shiny white 4x4, flinging week-old pizza boxes and sour milk cartons after him. I linger on the image of a blackened banana peel hanging off his bumper.

Next weekend, he can't take the kids. He wants me to tell them.

"You're better at this," he said, and I'd have taken it with a lot more grace if he hadn't been wearing a clean shirt and after-shave. Heading out for a hot date.

Tyler and Bethany dump their bookbags on the floor, crumpled drawings of Indians and turkeys, pages filled with long lines of crooked letters.

"Dad says we can get a puppy," Bethany says. Her smile is soft and dreamy. "I'm gonna name it Stardust."

"Bath time," I announce, and they pull long faces but giggle later in the tub. Once they're in bed, I mop up the wet floor and step outside for a smoke.

It's cold out, and the sky is filled with stars. I drag deep on the cigarette, exhaling anger along with the nicotine and tar. A puppy in that little apartment. How's he going to keep up with a puppy when he can't seem to keep up with anything else? Jenny would say, save the anger, store up the resentment as long as you can, warehouse the rage. "Takes a lot of adrenaline, honey, to keep up the fight." She ought to know. I can see lights on at her house, Wayne's car in the drive. Raised voices match angry shadows at the living room window, and I wonder what they're arguing about now. His child support payments, always late? Another missed court date? "Don't even try to be reasonable or nice," she always says. "They're just waiting for that. The law's on the side of the one who can stick it out. Ain't nobody looking out for you now, baby, but you."

I know that she's right. Sometimes the only thing that keeps me from sucking my thumb is the pain when I bite, tweaking my anger to keep it red-hot. How else to deal with broken promises and lame excuses and all his stupid lies? How else to handle letters from my lawyer on the six most urgent steps to extricate my credit history from the steaming pile of Dan's debts? The books say get over it, be civilized. Yeah, right. What I'd really like is to shake him up, let him find out I'm not so predictable, that I have the capacity for hate. Maybe if I'd done that sooner, he wouldn't have brought another woman to our bed. Other *women.*

My cigarette is down to the filter. I toss it away and stand for a moment at the edge of the porch. Smells like snow soon. All along the street, windows are lit against the dark, and I can see one patch of light after another, rooms with people inside. What did they do right? And what did I do that was so wrong? Where did I fail to keep my family intact? What goddamned rule did I break? It's not fair. It's not *fair,* but that's a child's word, a concept as substantial as fog. I don't know how to do this. I wasn't trained for divorce.

Jenny's house is silent and dark. Wayne's car is still in the drive, and I can't believe she'd just let him stay. "No sleeping with the enemy," I whisper as I turn to go in. "Don't be a traitor to your kind."

Tyler is cranky in the morning, and Bethany can't find her shoes. We race around gathering up papers and coats, bring Pop-Tarts and bananas into the car. As I turn the corner onto Davidson, a police cruiser comes up the block.

"Rrrrr," Tyler says as flashing lights go by. "I'm going to eat you."

At the office I feel a semblance of control, but hitting the grocery store as I leave work just about saps the last of my strength. I roll the cart up and down aisles, buying fish sticks and raisins and boxes of juice. Our family cuisine has fallen to the level of a five-year-old, but it's easier than pretending nothing's changed.

51

Sometimes I'd like to simply drop the facade. To rid myself of the American dream and just have us live in a tent like gypsies. Instead I listen to the experts, try to keep the kids' lives much the same, try to do the damn thing right. I'm going stone-broke, doing it on my own, and the house is too full of memories. Not only of what was, but what should have been. A family of four sitting at the dining room table, eating pot roast and apple pie. Or fajitas and beans. Or even Kentucky freaking Fried Chicken, so long as we were all there together. But it won't happen now, and it will never happen now, and I hate him, and I pretty much hate myself.

I round the last aisle and head for check-out, and then I see Dan. He's standing in the Ten Items or Less line, and I look at his cart. Motor oil, deli sandwich, a six-pack of beer. I wonder what he does at night in that bare-bones apartment, those quiet rooms. Watch TV? Sedate himself with a hundred and four channels, ESPN and Michelob longnecks? Does he watch sitcoms where single dads have wisdom and wit, or is it action movies with good guys and bad guys and no quarter given? Does he have regrets? I have no idea. Dan sees me, and all the light goes out of his eyes, and it's strange how much that hurts.

For a moment I consider going up another aisle, but then I remember Jenny and walk over to him. "*You* tell the kids about next weekend," I hiss at his shirt.

"No more dumping the dirty work. If you're going to let them down, then you have to bear the consequences. Not me."

"Oh, fine. I'll make them cry. Is that what you want? All men are bastards, right?"

"Not all men." I sense heads turning in our direction, but a reckless sense of power surges through my veins. "If you don't want to see people cry, stop whapping them across the face. Stop making stupid, useless promises and try doing what you're supposed to, just for the novelty of it. If you want to treat me like crap, that's one thing, but don't do it to your kids."

"Yeah, I'm the shit-king of the world, isn't that right? Remind me again." His voice is bitter, tight. "What's the matter, can't you even look me in the face?"

I wheel my cart around, go down to the other end of the check-out section. I can't. He's right. I can't look at his face, because I don't know who the hell he is any more.

It takes a long time to get the kids to bed. They're scared, upset, they don't understand. I don't understand either. Jenny's house is wrapped in crime tape: a black and yellow proclamation that something has gone terribly wrong. Wayne is dead, and Jenny's in jail. Revenge is an ugly word, but oh my god, she'd had that moment. That one victorious moment of knowing he felt the pain.

By midnight I've done all I can do. Folded laundry, paid bills, picked up toys and crayons and junk. For five minutes I stand at the end of my driveway, smoking a cigarette, looking at that dark house across the street. Finally, I throw the butt away and cross the line. Stepping over the tape, I creep up to the porch, cup my hands against the window. It's too dark to see in, and my breath steams up the glass. I can only imagine the scene. A black splotch on the floor, bits of blood and gore sprayed across the wallpaper and the curved-back couch. He used every possible loophole to dodge his responsibilities; she leveled the playing field with a vengeance. I wonder how he looked, whether his eyes were staring at the woman he never believed would stand up to him. Well, she did. It may not have been right, but perhaps it was fair. I don't know. I can't understand any more, can't make it register on my brain. Dan and I are through, we don't love, yet we are tied together as irrevocably as life and breath.

"Lady, step away from the house."

A police cruiser is shining a light on me. I turn and face it, hands balled into fists, my breathing ragged as if I'd been running a race. Raising my hands in a gesture of peace, that chump's refuge, I come slowly down the steps. I give name, address, apologize for trespassing. "It's just that I know those people. I feel bad for them. Do you know what's going to happen to her?"

His face is impassive, young. What does he know of heartache and loss? What does he know of that sensation of endlessly falling down the stairs, of constantly banging against the falsehoods of trust and fidelity? "I can't discuss it, Ma'am. You'd better go on home now. This is not a place you want to be."

I trudge back across the street, let myself in, knowing the officer is watching me turn on lights, close the door. I lock myself in so I won't run after him, banging on the trunk of his car, screaming at him about divorce laws and "justice" and how people manipulate it until it's no more than a twisted hunk of meddle.

In the bright light of the bathroom, it hits me what Jenny has done. She can't go backward from this, it's all gone too far, and for a minute my nostrils are filled with the scent of blood. Then I vomit, over and over, sinking to my knees on the cold floor. What am I doing? I can't go on with this anger clawing at my nerves; I can't go on hating the father of my children this way. Not when I have to see him every week, deal with him all the time. I can't go on being bitch to his bastard, harpy to his ass-holiness. It's killing me, not making me strong.

I'm shivering, shaking uncontrollably. I hate what I've become. I didn't want this. It wasn't on my agenda. I go to my room, crawl under the blankets. In the middle of the night, Tyler comes to my bed. "Scary people," he moans, and I take him in my arms, cuddle his round, flanneled body.

"It's okay," I tell him. "Mama's here. It was just a bad dream."

I have my own nightmare with which to contend. A vision of that other house behind the tape. I imagine lying on the floor in that darkened living room. Inches away from me, blackened gore reeks in a yellow patch of sunlight. I lie there, watching a fly wring his hands over so much blood, so little time. My children are sleeping in their beds. Tyler's is painted red and blue, with tiny motorcars glued to the headboard. Bethany's is pink. A Barbie fantasy of scallops and frills. I call, but they don't wake, and my voice wavers and echoes in a long hallway full of unopened doors.

Morning arrives like the US Calvary. I drink coffee, fix cereal, locate lost jackets and backpacks, herd the children out to the car. Bethany tells me, with great elaboration of gesture and voice, the continuing soap opera of the playground. Tyler is bright-eyed and eager this morning. He runs a HotWheel along the car window ledge. I start the engine and back out of my driveway, looking to my left at that silent house across the street. Then I look to the right and see my own house, with Tyler's trike still on the front lawn and Bethany's artwork in the window. It's their home, and I am the foundation. Tomorrow we'll rake leaves, go for a drive, eat hot dogs at a diner. Bethany will turn cartwheels on the front lawn. Tyler will learn to tie his shoes.

Life isn't going to be what I expected. Dan and I messed up. We took a good thing and turned it inside out, and now nothing fits. Bethany hums softly beside me as I head up the road into our day. Who would've thought that one November morning in my thirty-fourth year, I'd have to grow up?

Cubby Holes and Hiding Places

WHEN I WAS SIX, MY MOTHER would pin a pair of bed sheets to the clothesline and turn them into a tent for me. We'd pull the sheets out like a pair of wings, weigh down the corners with bricks, and spread an old quilt on the grass beneath. On hot summer days, I'd lay on the quilt, accompanied by several hairless dolls, and watch the patterns of clouds or leaves as the sun passed overhead. My bed sheet walls would billow lightly in the breeze, making me think of sailing ships and faraway adventures. The tent was my hiding place. Protected from the sun and the rude stare of passers-by, I could weave lovely daydreams for myself of princesses and goblins and rescuers on fine white horses.

When I was seventeen, I inherited my grandmother's desk. Antique cherry, with numerous cubby holes for important documents, and a hidden drawer. Here I kept my diary, full of such momentous statements as "Kevin said hi to me today." "Bought the new Beatles album." "Cut my hair." I enjoyed the act of sliding the secret panel back and reaching in for the leather diary and the accompanying velvet-covered jewelry box where I kept the key. I enjoyed even more the act of hiding the book again, closing the panel, locking the desk. No matter that my diary was full of mundane things. So long as the contents were hidden, I was a woman of mystique.

By the time I was thirty-six, my dreams were all for others. Good thing, since I had no privacy anyway, no secret spot that was mine alone. I shared my clothes with one daughter, my soft drinks with another. The baby seemed permanently attached to my breast while the toddler stayed clamped to my leg. If I had dreams for myself, they were only for a solid night's sleep.

When I was forty-six, my husband gave me a gazebo. It was a Mother's Day gift in a difficult year, when I was dealing with my parents' mortality. It's a lovely gazebo - octagonal, with a cedar-shingled roof, scallops and fretwork, a swing and benches. We placed it in our backyard, facing the lake, and surrounded it with azaleas and daylilies. I can sit out there and enjoy the view. Watch birds and ducks and geese, listen to the creak of the dock and water lapping at the pier. As evening falls, I can watch chimneysweeps wheel and glide. Even see an occasional small bat. It's not exactly private - any of my neighbors, glancing out, would see me sitting there - but there's a sense of isolation from the everyday world. No phone or TV, and I'm out of range to be bothered by teen-age bickering.

Yet I rarely sit there.

I thought about that yesterday, glancing through a magazine showing lovely porches and patios and gazebos just like mine. Photograph after photograph illustrated how one could design themselves a retreat, a refuge from the world, where all problems are solved with a cup of Café Amaretto and a good book. I could have that too. The autumn is an especially beautiful time out by the lake. The colored leaves reflect in the water, the sky is so blue. As evening falls, the lake turns purple, highlighted by a coppery reflection of the setting sun. I could sit out there in the gazebo and drink it all in, feel my soul relax and renew, but I don't.

Filled with a sense of time passing, I rush around on one task or another. Finish a project, clean a room, drive a child here or there. Busy busy busy. I've been in full forward movement so long, I'm not sure I know how to relax any more.

I want some time to think, to rest. I want to explore my cubby holes and hiding places and see what's in there. Which hidden worries, what hopeful dreams? I can't just jump into such thoughts, they have to be unearthed, pulled out of their hiding places, unlocked with some special key. I turn fifty this year. Pretty scary stuff, especially since I've seen my mother incapacitated since she was sixty-three. How much time do I have left for all the things I want to do?

And oh! I want them. With all the longing and yearning of a teenager, I want those dreams I still have. They're why I keep so busy, trying to cram the most into each day, afraid I'll get caught with so much yet undone. Afraid to take time, that precious gift, and waste it unproductively. Maybe I've been going about it all wrong. Maybe the gazebo is exactly what I need. A refuge where I can sit, to think. Even, perchance, to dream. Perhaps those magazine photos have it right - a steaming cup of coffee, some buttery cookies, and a fresh breeze off the lake - and above all, granting myself the right to take a little time to restore my soul. I believe I'll give it a try.

Don't Let Me Bother You

WHATCHA DOIN', KID?

I'm writing a paper, Gramps.

For school?

Yeah.

What's it about?

Irony.

That's a funny subject to be writing about. What kind of school is that?

Well, we're supposed to write a story with an ironic twist to it.

Oh! I thought you said ironing.

Oh, no Gramps, not ironing, irony, I-R-O-N-Y.

Well, that's good. Because you don't know nothing about ironing, that's for sure.

Very funny. Ha ha.

Yeah, I thought so. Well, don't let me bother you. I know you probably gotta concentrate.

Thanks, Gramps.

You know what's ironic?

What, Gramps?

That guy who won the lottery the other day. He's gonna get $4 million dollars and you know what, he's already rich. Now that's ironic.

Well, no, I don't think that's really ironic. You see, ….

No, what that is, is a crying shame. I had $20 on that lottery.

Oh, I'm sorry.

And here I sit…..well, don't let me bother you, I can see you're busy.

Thanks, Gramps.

I'm just waiting for your mother. She's s'posed to take me to the drugstore.

Okay, Gramps.

We gotta get my prescriptions. Derned pills. You take one to help your sugar diabetes and one to help your heart and one to help your blood pressure and then you take another one just so you can piss them all away again….Hey, now that's ironic!

Mmmm, I don't know.

And then you gotta pay the dern bill on top of it!

I hate it for you, Gramps.

I don't know what's taking your mother so long.

Prob'ly talking to your Aunt Linda again. Now there's irony for you. The two of them couldn't talk for five minutes without fighting when they were kids. Now that they live 200 miles apart, they gotta get on the phone and talk, talk, talk. And pay a dern dime a minute to do it. Don't know what they find to talk about all the time. Derned nuisance, the phone. Yadder, yadder, yadder. Don't know where they get it. Your grandma wasn't so talky like that. Well, don't let me bother you. I'll go see what's keeping your mother.

You know what I found your mother doing?
What?
She's cleaning the house.
Oh.
You know why?
Mmmm, no.
'Cos tomorrow the cleaning people are coming. You get that? She's cleaning the house so the cleaning people can clean. Now, THAT's ironic, kid.
Well, maybe. But mostly she's picking up so they can dust and vacuum, Gramps.
Seems derned ironic to me. And then she's gonna pay them. I told her, let me pick up and sweep and she can pay ME. Then I'd have some derned poker money!
Wouldn't that be a little difficult trying to clean while using the walker, Gramps?
Oh, that dern thing. I don't need that. I just use it to humor your mother.
Really?

Yeah, she thinks I need it.

But you don't?

Oh, I take it for a walk now and then……hey! Is that ironic? Well, don't let me bother you, I can see you're working away. That computer work good for you?

Yeah, it's great.

I don't like 'em. Rather have a handwritten letter any day. You can tell a lot about a person by their handwriting, you know. Can't tell a dern thing by typing – huh, except maybe if they can spell or not. Your grandmother had beautiful handwriting.

I remember.

She was a lovely woman. 50 years together and never a bad moment, not one! I hope you never forget her.

I won't, Gramps.

She could cook a peach pie that would make a dead man's mouth water, and as for her dumplings! Ooh, makes me ache right here thinking about 'em.

Yeah.

Well, don't let me bother you….I don't know what's keeping your mother so long.

Gramps? You ok?

Yeah….I was just thinking about your Grandma…..I was just thinking about how she used to like to write, too. Just like you. You remind me a lot of her, you know. Something about the way you hold your head, I don't know. And your eyes, so blue like hers. I

remember the first time I saw her, I thought I was
struck by lightning when I saw those blue eyes. Tried to
write a poem about them once.
You're kidding!
No, I really did try. Wasn't no good, though.
Did you show it to her?
Nah, she woulda laughed.
Oh, you should have shown it to her, she loved stuff
like that!
Nah.
Oh, Gramps, she would have loved it. You know how
she was always writing poems herself, remember? On
the backs of envelopes and little scraps of paper,
whatever she found….I even found a poem written in
her cookbook, once.
Well, I thought about it but never did show it to her.
That's too bad.

I stuck it in her coffin.
Huh?
The poem. I stuck it in her coffin.
Oh.
Well…..I figured she oughta have something of mine to
take with her.
I see. Well, I bet she was glad to have it.
Yeah, maybe…..well, don't let me bother you, kid.
You're not bothering me, Gramps.

Say It

BEN WORKS HORSES NOW. HE'S become muscular – arms carved and sinewy beneath his tan – and he smells like sweat. When we hold each other at night, I like to breathe in his scent, the tang of earth, the grounding we've found. We don't talk much about that day, dragging ourselves cold and almost lifeless from the sea, water streaming from our hair and eyes. Words aren't the only way to communicate and besides, there are better things to talk about.

At evening's end, when everyone else has gone inside and patches of light from the windows fall on the ground, I sit on the porch steps and remember. I can do that now, think about Josh, his little body curved and heavy, tiny hands reaching for me. I close my eyes and imagine his hair, how it smelled, how soft it felt against my cheek. My lips can almost feel the smooth warmth of his skin and for a brief moment, he's there in my arms. I'm glad I can remember him like this and I think, Someday. When Ben and I have grown up again.

Ben didn't mean to do it. That fact was clear from the start and even the police officers seemed sorry they had to question us over and over. I'd been home sick with the flu. Ben took Joshie to daycare but on the way, his thoughts began to focus on work, his veterinarian practice, and he forgot. He simply went to work and forgot.

At the hospital there were too many shocks. Ben, crying, apologizing as I hurried through the doors. "I'm sorry, I'm so sorry." Then seeing Josh, already stiffening, a stranger in my baby's clothes. I couldn't talk then and I couldn't talk later when they led Ben away, his face streaked white on white in reflection of rain on the squad car windows. By then, the rain fell steadily and already the temperatures had dropped twenty degrees. Twenty degrees, the difference maybe between life and death on a hot July afternoon in Atlanta. What if it had rained earlier? My mother came to get me, walked me to her car, drove out of the parking lot past Ben's crookedly parked black sedan. Just above the windowsill, I could see the ruffled edge of the quilt in Josh's car seat. I could imagine it, the limp body lifted, the horrified cry, the realization. Don't think about it, I told myself, don't picture it, don't.

Talk of charges gave way to whispers about suicide watches. They released Ben in time for the funeral and he showed up, pale and aged, his features softened and distorted as though he'd been underwater a long time. The priest reminded us that there is a reason for everything, to trust in God and believe. Believe what? I watched the candle flames. One of them kept flickering, caught perhaps in an unseen draft. Was there a reason for that too?

Afterward, people spoke to us. Ben's aunt urged me to seek counseling. "You need to talk about it, get your feelings out." I nodded, unable to meet her eyes, then made my way to the bathroom. There wasn't one useful thing in that cabinet. I finally took some Dramamine and it seemed to help. By evening, my stomach was so calm I could have driven off the edge of the world and never noticed.

When it was all over, Ben and I went home. Somebody had been in to clean up. The diaper pail was empty, even though I clearly remembered three wet diapers in the bottom of it that morning. Joshie's sleeper, too, had been washed out and put away. Ben began crying again and I had to undress him, put him to bed, stroke his hair until he fell asleep. This was my husband, the man with whom I was supposed to talk, open up, share my feelings. One wrong word would have killed him.

I've always tried to do the right thing, but what do you do when the right thing is all wrong? I needed someone to be there, to help me. Someone more capable, someone wise and noble, but I only had me.

For a few days we stumbled around the house, sleepwalkers. Ben talked about his practice, about going back. "What about my patients?" he asked. "Should I forget about them too?" Then his eyes filled again and he dropped to his knees, wrapping his arms around my legs. "Oh god, I'm so sorry. Tell me you hate me. Say it, I killed him. Say it." All I could think was, turn me loose. You're dragging me down, we'll both be lost. But instead I bent over him, stroked his back. Couldn't speak, still couldn't speak, words all slipped away from me like water through my fingers.

"Let's leave, get out of here," I finally said. The house suffocated me. "I don't care where, let's just go."

We drove for four days. Hit I-40 and followed it, straight as an arrow, to the coast. Ben slept most of the time and that was fine with me. The highway became our haven, long silent miles of concrete. Anonymous rest areas, homogenous truck stops. Meals of mashed potatoes and meatloaf, banana cream pie. Familiar tastes swallowed with ease, settling in our stomachs like pap. I popped Dramamine, my new drug of choice. We stayed in Red Roof Inns and a Motel 6. At night, Ben clung to the edge of the mattress, rolled into a ball, endlessly rocking himself to sleep. I lay awake, staring at the ceiling, my gut twisting tighter and tighter.

It was raining when we reached the beach. Children and parents had deserted the sands, sprinting for their cars with towels flapping. We walked out on the pier, hand in hand. Hurrying now, I jerked at Ben's arm and he stumbled along, docile as a child, not speaking a word. I was deaf by then anyway and the fog muffled sound. There'd be no sound ever again, if I'd had my way about it. No angry words, no recriminations or endless apologies. No truths, no lies.

Ben's fingers tightened, interlocking with mine and we stared out at the sea, dark waves under the seamless gray sky. The water would be cold, and I welcomed the thought of smooth oblivion. We swung our linked hands back and forth, as though there were a small child between us, squealing with pleasure as his feet left the ground.

For one moment, we were free. Soaring as we left the earth's tug, and then down we fell into the screaming cold. Not the calm I'd expected. We were thrown, tossed, pulled apart. We scrabbled at each other, clawed and snatched, pushed, kicked, fought. My face broke free of the waves and I got one gasping lungful of air before I started to sink again. Ben thrashed alongside, reaching for my hand and I thought, *you forgot our child.* I brought my feet up, thrust them against his chest, and pushed hard, forcing myself away.

Ben works horses now, and I clean and cook. Driving back from the coast, not wanting to go home and not knowing where else to go, we stopped for a meal in Cuervo, New Mexico, and saw the Help Wanted sign. It's a small ranch, nothing fancy, and we're just hired hands, but it's enough. Late in the afternoons, before I prepare mountains of fried chicken and biscuits, gallons of tea, I hang laundry under the sun. The sky is wide here and it goes from edge to edge.

Wind blows endlessly, carrying red flakes of dust that cling to the shirts and towels and I beat them off with an old tennis racket I've found. It's a satisfying task, backswing and forehand, long arcs of strength. With each swing, there's a resounding thwack and dust leaps off, glad to be out of the line of fire.

The tennis racket doesn't belong there at all, any more than we do, but it does the job. I fold sheets and faded jeans, hold them close to my face for a moment, and lay them in the basket. The racket I toss in the air, watching the handle and webbed head rotate end over end, silhouetted against the purple sky. I reach my hand out and the wood drops solidly into my palm. We did everything wrong, Ben and I. But somehow, it turned out all right.

Room 506, Bed 2

She's our Mom.
She is not a stroke,
Or a subdural hematoma,
Or a bad heart valve.
She's our Mom.
And we loan her to you on the understanding
That you are now on her team.

She loves old movies,
Manicures and pedicures,
And having dinner out.
She's a Skip-Bo fiend.

When you ask her complaints,
She will smile and say she's fine,
Except she doesn't understand why her fingers are
numb,
And her handwriting's so bad,

And she can't remember any of her grandchildren's
names,
Although she knows who they are.
She'll ask how you are, too.

She'll be an easy patient, undemanding, quiet.
She will do whatever the doctor says.
We, however, will be in and out, asking questions,
Wanting to know, keeping vigil in the night,
We will be in pain.

So we enter into this bargain with you,
You who care for the sick, the aged.
You who have the training and skill.
We'll loan her to you for a short time.
We will keep the appointments and follow your guide.
And you will remember she's our Mom.
And she's more than the sum of her parts.

Another Weekend with Susie

MY SISTER HAS TURNED INTO a bag lady. There's no getting around it. That's how she looks as she gets off the plane, dressed in an old knit hat that's pulled down to the tops of her eyeglasses, a too-big man's coat and orthopedic shoes. She gives me a tight hug, hurting my neck with her stiff-armed grip, and heads for the baggage pickup area. She has no time for idle chitchat. There's a suitcase to retrieve. For this, I used up one of my sick days from work.

We get in the car, and I turn on the radio as soon as we're rolling. Susie's lips begin to move, and I crank up the sound a little. I don't like to listen to her talk to herself. I don't like to hear the strange things she says, and, I suppose, she's entitled to her privacy.

It's an hour to the retirement center where Mom lives now. I turn off the engine before Susie expects it, and her monologue runs over. ...*sack of shit,* I hear her say.

Mom is so happy to see her. She hugs Suzie and tries to find a place for us to sit. All the chairs in Mom's little room are covered with stacks of magazines, mostly supermarket tabloids or celebrity gossip rags. Mom can't read any more, but she likes the pictures.

Susie removes her coat and hat. Her hair is dirty, and she wears it in a braid down her back. Her plaid shirt clashes with her striped pants. Mom asks her, as she always does, why she doesn't wash her hair more often. I don't say anything. Mom's trousers are on backwards. The two of them are starting to be a matched set. I would kill for a Coke.

We try to have conversation, exchange personal news. There really isn't any; we talk to each other at least once a week. But it's too early to go to lunch.

"Do you remember John Sparks?" Susie asks mom. "He's in my group at school. Do you remember him? You danced with him at the last Family Weekend." Susie peers at Mom through her thick glasses. The frames are cheap-looking. We have to replace them so often that we don't get the good kind any more. The Voices keep telling her to throw them out.

"John who?" my mother asks.

"You danced with him, remember? He had a limp."

"Did you go to a dance? When was that, Honey?"

"No, Mom, *you* danced—last year at the Family Weekend."

"Whose family? When was that?"

"Last year, Mom. Anyway, he had surgery on his hip."

"Surgery? When did you have surgery?"

"Oh, never *mind*."

Maybe it's not too early to go to lunch.

*****

We sit in the corner booth at Applebee's. She reads over every word in the menu and finally orders, as I knew she would, the Veggie Patch pizza and a milkshake. She always orders the same thing. She says the food at school is OK, but there's not enough pizza. We call it her School, like she's going to college or something, but it's really a group home for schizophrenics. Mom orders spaghetti and when it comes tries to eat it with her spoon. I take the spoon away and give her the fork, making sure the tines are turned the right way. Susie sits stiffly, staring at nothing, her eyes dilated and her lips moving. She eats mechanically, wiping her mouth with her napkin between each bite.

I wipe spaghetti sauce off Mom's hand and sleeve and ask Susie what she's been up to. She shrugs and says she's too tired to do much.

"I just stay in my room and watch my videos. And write."

"What do you write?" Mom asks. *Don't ask*, I silently beg her, *you know what she writes*. Susie's face clicks shut.

"How about dessert?" I say brightly, and they perk up. They both order ice cream sundaes, despite the fact that Susie has already had a milkshake. She has an insatiable void she keeps trying to fill.

"I'm getting married in August," Susie announces. "To Tony Poletti."

"Tony Poletti who goes to my church?" I ask. "Don't you think that will be quite a surprise to his wife?"

"She isn't really his wife."

"Whose wife?" Mom asks.

"Tony Poletti's wife," I say. "And what about his five kids?"

"I like kids."

"Whose kids?" Mom asks.

"Tony Poletti's kids," I say. "Is it going to be a white wedding? Can I be the maid of honor?" I shouldn't egg her on this way. Dr. Cavanaugh says when she makes outrageous statements, the best thing is to let them lie, but honestly, sometimes it's so funny I just have to laugh. Besides, I have so few hobbies.

Susie gets pissed. "I *am* getting married to Tony in August, and then we are going to live on an Indian Reservation in Arizona with my tribe!"

It's interesting that just two or three decibels of sound can take a voice from normal to attention-getting loud. The women at the next table start to snicker.

"Susie," I say in my quiet, slightly sad voice designed to induce guilt. She puts her glasses back on. "It's time to take Mom home." Susie helps wipe Mom's hands and face, solicitously takes her to the Ladies' Room, and waits patiently while I pay the bill.

*****

"What did you say?" Mom asks. We're in the car and Mom always makes me turn off the radio when she's with me. Susie's voice has been soft, but not soft enough. "Are you talking to yourself again?"

"Yes, Mom," Susie says tiredly. "I do that." Mom asks her again what she said and Susie refuses to reply. I reach over and press Mom's hand and she shuts up, but she fidgets restlessly when we hear the soft hiss of Susie's whispers.

We take Mom back to her room. It's time for Suzie's medicine, and I watch her take the pills—orange, green, pink. Anti-depressant, anti-psychotic, anti-convulsant. I have another Coke, my own drug of choice. Susie is restless, not interested in the photo albums that Mom wants to show us. I wish Mom would put them away. It depresses me to see the old pictures of Susie as a cheerleader, a high school

79

graduate, with her first car. Susie reminds me that I promised to take her to the mall to get more notebooks.

"What you need to get," Mom admonishes her, "is some clothes. There's plenty of money in your account. You should buy yourself some nice things. Get some pretty Spring clothes while you're here." Susie's bottom lip thrusts out, and I intervene.

"Well, there's lots of stores to choose from at the mall, Mom. I'm sure Susie can find whatever she wants." I peek at Susie from under my bangs. She half-smiles back. It's the old game of Us vs. Authority. When we get to the store, Susie buys Native American music and videos. I buy her a pair of silver and turquoise earrings as a gift. Susie's most prevalent delusion is that she is a Cherokee native. I don't know why.

In the electronics section, her attention is pulled to a box with a picture of a CD player. The box is brightly colored in a geometric pattern, and she stares at it. We stand there for almost 10 minutes. I pretend I'm looking for some elusive cassette. Her lips move, and she suddenly laughs loudly. "Susie!" I whisper harshly, and she turns towards me. Her expression is flat, but she behaves, and we walk over to the stationery supplies. She loads up on notebooks, the 5-subject kind only, and buys dozens of pens. A woman goes by with a baby in her shopping cart, and Susie looks after her, eyes suddenly filled with tears. Concerned, I touch her arm.

"It's not true," she whispers. "I'm *not* a whore, like she says."

"That woman didn't say anything, Suze." I pat her arm. Sometimes I can't stand the things the Voices say to her. "I know you're a good person."

Susie slowly pushes the cart. She rests her elbows and forearms on the handle and hunches her shoulders. Gradually she works her way into her CP walk, hands twisted and curled, one foot dragging. She doesn't really have cerebral palsy, and it irritates me when she does this.

"If you're too tired, we should go home," I warn her. She straightens up. Hurrying now, she throws M&Ms, caramel corn and soft drinks into the cart. We're almost done. One last item, henna rinse, and we can go to the checkout stand. I look at my manicure with regret; it will be ruined by tonight's haircoloring job.

My husband is already home when we get there. He has started dinner for me and has gotten the kids to set the table. I must be looking a little wild-eyed by now—he's overly hearty in his greetings to Susie. All the shopping bags go to her room with her, and I know she won't come out again until she's called. My husband offers me an aspirin.

We finish fixing dinner, and I put away laundry while the children play outside. When I walk past her room, I can hear Susie talking loudly. *You look so gorgeous!* she says, but not to me.

*****

Susie has two helpings of everything at dinner and three glasses of iced tea. My older daughter begins wiping her mouth with her napkin after every bite, and my younger daughter begins to snicker.

I give them a fierce look, and they giggle at each other. I can't make them stop without drawing their behavior to Susie's notice. I can feel the anger turn white behind my eyeballs. God, when I think of all those times on the junior high school bus, when some stupid kid would be giving me a hard time, and Susie would stand up for me, and now I can't even protect her from being mocked by my own children.

"Leave the table!" I mouth at them, and they sober up. Sometimes, I hate kids.

Susie's eyes gleam, and she has an enormous smile on her face. I often picture her Voices as being like someone standing right behind her shoulder, whispering in her ear. When she smiles like this, I think that one of the Voices must be telling her in-jokes, like having your own private David Letterman. She laughs out loud, and the kids stare at her and then at me.

Sometimes I hate Susie.

*****

It's bedtime, and I'm exhausted. Susie spent most of the evening in my bedroom with the door shut, watching her new videos on my TV. This makes my husband antsy, but it's better than trying to make conversation with her. I tell him about the Tony Poletti story.

"What do you think she'll do when August comes?" he asks. I just shrug. Susie always finds a reason why these fantasies don't come true. My husband leaves, and I clean up the mess from the henna rinse. Susie comes into the kitchen, admiring her newly darkened hair in a hand mirror.

"Remember the time I cut your hair?" she asks. I laugh. It had been a classically botched job. Susie holds one lock of her hair up at an angle and smirks at me. I laugh again, then snort accidentally. We both crack up, and I remind her of the time the family was on a trip, and she kept farting so bad that we all had to roll down the car windows, despite a driving rain. We're laughing so hard that my husband comes to see what's the matter. Just as he walks in, Susie cuts a fart—a real cheek-slapper—and we practically fall down on the floor, crying with laughter. My husband just shakes his head and walks out of the room.

"Oh brother," I say, "those were the good old days, weren't they?" We hug each other goodnight. I am still giggling a little as I go down the hall. When I look back, Susie is staring at herself in the hall mirror. Her lips are moving. I stop laughing.

*****

A family friend has offered to have Susie spend Saturday with her. I gratefully accept, and Susie is happy to go. I do my usual Saturday chores—laundry, cleaning, shopping. I remember to get Mom's drycleaning and her special diet soda. I pay the bills. I write checks for Mom's bills out of her account, and I write checks for Susie's bills out of a special trust account.

Susie comes home all happy and excited. Our friend, Loretta, has had an idea. What about taking Susie to the beach this summer? I explain that Susie's school offers trips to various places, but Susie always declines.

"That's because she doesn't want to go with the others at the school. She wants to go with her family! Why don't you just rent a cottage for a week? You could bring your Mother, too." I stare at Loretta. *Have you lost your mind?* Then I remember, Loretta's the one who had the hot idea of the henna rinse two years ago, and now every time Susie comes home, I have to go through the whole mess.

"It would be great!" Susie enthuses. She squeezes my son around his shoulders. "I could play on the beach and help you guys make sandcastles. I have enough money," she suddenly pleads with me. "I could pay my own way."

I stare at her. I think maybe I have died and gone to hell. How can I tell her no? But how can I tell her yes? I remember other times, trips that turned into fiascos. The time Susie locked herself in the gas station bathroom and wouldn't come out for two hours. The poor guy in Toronto that she accused of raping her.

I give a dirty look to Loretta. "I don't think Mom could go. Can you just see her trying to walk on the beach with her cane?" Loretta looks back at me blandly.

"Well, just take your sister," she concedes.

"Thanks for having Suze over," I say and take Loretta's elbow, guiding her to the door. She smiles at me, and I pinch her arm and give her a fierce look. "Sorry you can't stay," I say, and I refrain from pushing her down the steps.

I turn back to Susie. She still has her arm around my son's shoulders. He makes a comic face at me, and she grins smugly. The dryer buzzer sounds and I go to the laundry room, where I pull clothes out of the machine like I'm pulling hair. Damn it, damn, damn, *damn*.

*****

"I can cut it myself!"

Mom grabs the knife from Susie and starts sawing away at her steak. It would seem more defiant if she didn't have the blade turned wrong side up. Susie sighs loudly and frowns at her soft drink. I look out the window.

"That was a pretty good movie," Susie says. "I liked that actor who played the boyfriend."

"Now which one was the boyfriend again?" Mom asks. The blonde one, I tell her.

"I thought the blonde was a girl."

"That was the *other* blonde. Geez, Mom, the blonde with the deep voice was the boyfriend."

Susie grins at me. I roll my eyes, and we both laugh a little. Mom slept through most of the movie anyway—there is no way to fill her in on the whole thing now. We finish our meal and take Mom home. As we turn to go, Mom hugs Susie tightly.

"Have a safe trip," she murmurs into Susie's neck. "See you in August." We walk down the hall and turn back to look at Mom in the doorway of her room. She looks small and crumpled.

We get in the car, and I ask Susie how Mom seems to her.

"Pretty good, considering." Susie reaches to turn the radio on, but I stop her. Does she see much change in Mom?

"Yes, of course I do. What do you want me to say?" She reaches for the radio again, and I allow her to turn it on. Her voice whispers and mutters just below comprehension level. When I stop at a red light, I hear *...hate her...* and I wonder whether she's talking about me or Mom. Or God knows whom.

We walk into the darkened house. Susie asks for something cold to drink, and I pour it for her.

"I could get married, you know," she says, her eyes flickering over at me. "I have money, and I could get married and move into Mom's old house."

I lean against the counter and fold my arms. I look her straight in the eye and ask if Tony Poletti is still her man.

She shrugs and pouts. "I just want a family. You have one. Why can't you understand that I want one. I can take care of kids." She looks at me slyly. "I know how to make a man happy. You think I don't."

Zing! The blood jumps inside me.

"I could help with Mom," she whines. "Let me move home, and I'll take care of her. She wouldn't have to live at the retirement center any more, and you wouldn't have to sell the house."

I'm so tired. I go into the living room and lie on the couch. Susie follows me, hammering away at her theme, her fists clenched. "It's not fair!" she shouts. "I'm the oldest. You can't always tell me what to do!"

"Fine," I tell her. "Do what you want. In fact, I'll trade places with you. I'll go to your school and go on all those trips you don't want to make and have someone cook and clean for me. You stay here. You take care of Mom. Fill out all those insurance forms. Take her to all her doctor appointments, do her taxes. Keep the damn house. Just be sure to get the exterminator over there soon—there's an infestation of spiders! And don't forget, you'll need to keep Mom's medicines straight—she takes 14 pills a day." I swing my legs over the edge of the couch and sit up. "And when she dies, you can have the pleasure of doing all the funeral arrangements like I did for Dad. *Be my guest!*" I spit at her. "Believe me, I'll be happy to go back to my rightful place as the spoiled brat baby sister!"

"Just do me one favor," I yell as I leap to my feet. "Don't be asking me for any help. I've done it for ten years. I'll be fucking glad to let you take the next ten!"

Susie stands there blinking. She opens her mouth, but before she can say anything, my husband comes into the room.

"That's enough!" he yells. "You two just stop it! Just shut the hell up!"

Susie stalks off to her room. I shut myself in the bathroom, waiting to stop shaking. Finally, I climb into bed, and my husband puts his arms around me. "Rebecca, you can't go on like this," he says sharply, but I know his anger is over his inability to help. That is when I start to cry, choking and shuddering until he almost gives up trying to calm me. Finally, I wipe my eyes and try to sleep. I can't sleep, of course, and just stare into the darkness, consumed with grief, guilt and self-pity. I can't go on like this, for sure, but what the hell choice do I have?

*****

Sunday morning, and we go to church. Susie sits up straight and alert. She likes going to Mass. After Mass, several of the parishioners who remember Susie stop to say hello. She basks in the attention, and I watch to see if she gives Tony Poletti a special greeting. He gives her one of his usual bear hugs, and she smiles beatifically at him. *If he only knew,* I think, and I have to hide my grin.

We have lunch at home, cooking hamburgers on the grill. Susie sits on the swing, gazing at the fields below our house. I'm busy setting the picnic table and helping with the food, but I watch her. Her back is slumped. One foot trails back and forth as the swing moves. She'll never have a normal life. She'll never have a husband or a baby. Her only real friend is the one who whispers in her ear, but it is a fickle friend, quick to turn on her.

"Look at my new baseball glove," my son says and shows her his finest possession.

"I used to play baseball," she tells him. He gives her a skeptical look, and she assures him, "Yes, and I roller-skated and rode my bike. I used to do lots of things." She turns and looks at me, and I find that I have to go into the house for a minute.

I drive her to the airport. The radio is on low, and Susie's whispers hiss without pause. She is in high gear once we get there, loping through the airport, checking her luggage, displaying the school-issued identification badge to the gate agent at the counter. She has no driver's license any more, and it used to embarrass her to have to wear her ID on a chain around her neck, but today she flashes it around like a boy with his first moustache.

We have to wait. We arrived too early. She taps her fingers on her purse. I leaf through a magazine.

Finally, I say it. "I'm sorry. I shouldn't have yelled at you. I know it's hard for you to always have to be away from home."

She looks at me. Her eyes are dilated, and her lips are moving. Then she focuses on me and smiles. She has a very sweet smile. "It's ok", she says. "I know I'm better off at school. It's just that sometimes I want things, you know?"

I have no answer. There is no answer. The agent announces the boarding of Susie's flight, and Susie turns to me for a hug. I fumble as I give her the little travel case and drop my purse. Susie picks it up and gently puts the strap back on my shoulder, smoothing my collar. Then we hug, and she trudges off to the plane. I often wonder what her fellow passengers make of her whispering to herself. Maybe they just think she's a white-knuckle flier.

I get into the car to drive home, the radio off, the fresh air sliding through the windows. I think about this morning, cleaning out the room Susie used, the dozens of crumpled pages I fished out of the wastebasket, covered with her deeply slanting scrawl. *I love you I will be with you, have a chip on your shoulder, don't you. We will live together and I will be Indian too damned devil worshipper I will cook I will marry an Indian brave we will be married in August there is no reason to blame me, why do you blame me! I can drive I can be good wife grandmother of all...*

I know I shouldn't read these letters. They are so filled with a combination of longing and madness that they tear me up. I wonder if they help her to hold it together in public by letting it out in private.

Tomorrow I go back to my nice, orderly office. Susie will return in three months, and we'll have good times and bad times. I try not to mourn for the sister I once had. I deal with the sister I've got, and she, in her own way, deals with me. I guess that's about par for the course.

Water's Edge

ON THE LAST DAY OF SUMMER in his 82nd year, Rafe Abernathy opened the screen door and stepped quietly out on his daughter's back porch. The air was still, breathless in the late-day sun, and the grass was parched, crackling underfoot as he walked to the dock. The weathered pier, silver-gray and warped, swayed slightly as he trod its length, groaned and creaked as he climbed down into his fishing boat. He leaned forward and let the wad of tobacco roll out of his mouth and fall into the water. Digging in his pocket for the little pouch of Red Man, he stared at the lake a minute, lost in thought. Finally, he tore off a new wad and stuffed it into his cheek, low against the gum, where its sweet burn felt so familiar.

Back in the house, his sons and daughter talked on and on. His daughter's voice, heavy with shoulds and have-tos, faded to little more than a mosquito's whine.

Let them talk. He saw no need for change, and their worrying wore him out.

He pulled off his shoes and left them on the dock, stowing his fishing pole, tackle box, and bait in the boat. The aluminum boat was a good one, he'd had it for twenty years. He cranked the motor with a pull on the flywheel, gripping the rope, jerking it just right so that the engine caught first try. It was good for a man to use his arm muscles now and then, even in his old age. The motor started, smooth and pretty, and he backed away from the pier in a long, slow arc. The fierce heat of the day was receding as the sun took a dip in the lake. Turning his face to catch the wind, Rafe breathed in the smell of fresh water, engine fumes and a trace of his fishing bait that always made him feel alive. In the evenings he liked to fish in the cove off Little Mountain Creek. It was quiet there, away from the dam and rough waters, and he didn't have to fight the kids on their jet skis and wave runners. He felt drowsy and even thought for a minute about stretching out in the bottom of the boat, letting the water rock him to sleep. It took so damned long to die, he was tired of it. Seemed like there could have been a better plan than this, something clean and dignified. Not these little insults - having bits of his body quit on him, so that he was barely treading water, being slowly forced against the wall of the inevitable.

The fishing line tightened and he pulled in a nice striped bass. Almost three pounds, he figured, pretty good. The fish struggled a moment and stopped, one eye on Rafe, gills opening and closing without choice. Rafe carefully removed the hook and put the fish back in the water. He held it underwater for a second, giving it a chance to figure things out, and then released it, watching it give a quick flip of its tail before it disappeared. "Go home," he said.

The day was fading. He revved up the engine and shot, a pure clean line, across the lake toward home. As he neared Blue Spring Cove, he slowed down. It was right about here, somewhere around here. Twenty, maybe thirty feet down was all. If the water was clearer, maybe he could have seen it, the foundations of the old place. Not much of a difference between being submerged and staying high and dry, a matter of just a few feet.

He was sixty years old the summer that he lost both his wife and his farm. His farm died slowly, foot by foot as the lake rose and water lapped at his cornfield, his kitchen garden, and the handmade bricks used in the foundations of the house built by his daddy in '22. His wife died quickly, between one breath and the next, a single bloodclot stopping an artery more efficiently than the dam blocked the river. Rafe didn't have much to say after that.

He never blamed the lake, it wasn't the lake's fault. The dam was built and the river kept flowing through the Piedmont, fed by countless streams and winter snows until it backed up into the valley. Water must find the lowest point, the ultimate home. His wasn't the only farm sacrificed, but it felt that way. The waters rose, covering pastureland and red clay roads, stumps of trees. The tiny crossroads town was lost, churches and cemeteries relocated, acres of rich bottomland were submerged. People would drive out on Sundays, picnicking in the fields and comparing notes about how much the lake had swallowed that week.

He missed the river, missed its drive and turbulence. A river has a reason, a life force, it *does* something. A lake was a good thing, a fine place for fishing, but he remembered the river.

It was the river that brought him Mae. The first time he saw her, she was being baptized in the river and the sight of her long white dress, clinging to her wet legs and breasts, had brought him to his knees. Their children were raised at the river's edge, dandled in the shallow pools, taught its mysteries. Mae and the river were so much alike, blessed coolness and relief after a day in the fields, where the sun was so hot and the heat rose above him in shimmering waves like the buzzing of insects. Mae's smile, and her chicken-fried steak, that was something to come home to. He could almost see her sometimes, moving around in the kitchen, the window shades pulled against the sun, her feet bare on the wood floor.

Rafe stared at the water. Copper lights from the sunset now streaking the sky played off the dark purple of the surface. A mallard quacked once nearby. He closed his eyes and pictured Mae, turning toward him with her slow smile, her body that gave him so much comfort all those years ago. He could almost smell the talcum she wore.

He should be going back.

Rafe sat there, elbows on knees, his eyes closed. All around him, night was settling in, noises muting, sky growing darker until a fine, needle-like rain began to fall, warm as bathwater. He continued to sit until he was just a dark shadow in a gray world, the sky and water merging in a silvery shroud, a still life of a still life.

Pinpoints of light edged the shoreline, lit-up windows with people inside. Somewhere along there was his daughter's kitchen. His children sitting around the table, talking, talking. Deciding things for him, without him. Choosing his future from a mess of brochures.

There was a splash in the water as a fish jumped nearby. Rafe stared at his hand, an old man's hand, fingers thick and blunt, curved with years of work. When did it get so old? He pushed his hand into the lake, the water streaming back between his fingers, giving a slight resistance that was sweet to contemplate. Rafe set down his pole, balancing the rod so that it wouldn't tip and fall. Carefully, for fear of dumping his tackle box, he slid over the side of the boat into the lake. Smooth, soft as a woman's embrace, the warm water received him, like sleep receives the dreamer. Face first, he pushed downward, his eyes searching. A slipstream of bubbles flowed over his body, tugged at his clothes and hair. The water seemed to push him up, force him to the surface, and he kicked harder and harder until, with a gasp, he burst downward out of the darkness.

In the pale gray light, shapes emerged. There was the old road, the red clay rising in a slurry, thick and spongy. The fence posts shone ghostly in the water, guiding his way. He could see the fields, cornstalks waving in the current. Watermelons bobbed in the kitchen garden, tethered by the vines.

He floated for a minute, figuring things out. Then, with a kick of his feet, he went in, slow and easy, sliding through an open window. His hair changing direction with each movement like a school of fish, his shirt rippling, he moved weightlessly into the room. The old photos framed on the wall leaned slightly forward, as if in surprise. A jug of daisies weighted down a doily, lace edges straining upward from the oak table. Pushing off from the doorjamb with his feet, Rafe glided into the kitchen.

She'd been cooking, he could tell in an instant. A plate of biscuits floated past. He reached out and took one, laughing to himself that he'd always said they were lighter than air. His chuckle sounded deep and bass, far away, a tuba in a marching band on the other side of the square. Treading water, turning in a slow spin, he searched the room for her, watched for the flash of a blue dress, a warm smile. Though his mouth was open, his tongue felt dry, parched, thirsty for what she alone could give him, thick with the long slow desire of years alone.

A bluegill swam through the room, darting off to the left past the china cupboard and then he saw her, one hand on the knob of the multi-paned cabinet door, the other placing a single cup back on its hook. She turned and looked at him, her eyes blue as ever, her dark hair caught in a ribbon the color of forsythia in the spring.

Rafe let his feet slide down, touch lightly on the wooden floor. "I'm home," he said, and the words floated out of his chest and lay like a benediction on the wall above her head. "I'm home."

***

The empty boat was found rocking aimlessly in the morning light. The coast guard auxiliary figured that maybe he'd fallen overboard, gotten confused in the dark.

His daughter, a sturdy matron with grandchildren of her own, told them he'd always been one to do things his own way, they'd been worried about him for some time. She never could keep him from going fishing after dark. "Seems like all he cared about was being out on that lake," she said. "I think it was the thing he loved the most." Rafe's shoes sat out on the dock for another month or so, unnoticed, curved with the shape of the old man's feet, until one night they, too, disappeared into the lake.

Geezer Wannabe

VIOLENCE FLARED TODAY at the Spartanburg, SC, office of the AARP when it was revealed that Mr. Ralph Goforth, of Reeps Grove Church Road, lied about his age on his membership application.

"I had my doubts about him all along," said Darryl Turbyfil, office manager. "He seemed just too anxious about signing up. Most people, you know, hate to admit they're 50. Turns out that dadblamed fool is only 39."

Some suspect it was the discounts that lured him into falsifying his records. "What else could it be?" asked Myra Hovis, of BettyBee's Hairstyles, across the street. "Good lord, I wouldn't be bragging that I was old, if I was still 39. I mean, when I *turn* 39. Um, I have to go now…"

Mr. Goforth admits that he was trying to fool people but denies the charge that it was over money. "I feel older than dirt," he said. "People always say, you're as old as you feel. Well, dang it, I *feel* fifty. Look at this!" Mr. Goforth whipped off his baseball cap and pointed out what was undeniably a receding hairline. "Besides, I own my own business. That's aged me at *least* 10 years, and my joints are starting to report in whenever I move. Doesn't that count?"

The truth came out when Mr. Goforth was signing up for the Bingo-a-Thon

held every Tuesday night. Long lines of bona fide AARP members overheard when the clerk asked him to spell his name and he shouted, "*No*, that's G as in Lady *GaGa*".

"He shot a look at the crowd and tried to fix it," reported Bobby Dean Hoyle,

of Hoyle's Oil. "Tried to say he meant G as in Bobby Goldsboro but the jig was up. Got kinda ugly there, we had a regular stampede of walkers and wheelchairs chasing him up the hall. He runs good, that fellow. Would have got clean away if he hadn't got knee-capped by Old Man Whitaker's cane."

Mr. Goforth was treated and released from the Spartanburg General Hospital and given a warning by Darryl Turbyfil of AARP. "I don't know what it is lately," Mr. Turbyfil sighed. "This isn't the first case I've seen. Something just seems to come over men when they hit 39. Maybe it's true that we older guys do exude a kind of sophistication. But don't let our gray hairs and bifocals fool you, it's not *all* glamour. We fifty-year-olds have our insecurities too. We know we won't be fully acceptable as geezers for at least 15 more years."

Mr. Goforth has refused further comment. He is sequestered at the home of his sister, Miss Debbie Goforth of Sunbeam Drive. "I hope y'all realize that Ralph's a little demented," she said. "There's no way that he's 50. After all, I'm only 25 myself." This reporter has declined to comment.

Seven Warning Signs
That Will Save Your Life

THE "SAFE IN THE CITY" CLASS MEETS in the basement of the United Methodist church in a meeting room where the bulletin boards are covered with Boy Scout Badge posters and parish clean-up schedules. Gina promised her mother she'd take the class, and it is probably a good idea, but she never thought she'd be spending her Tuesday evenings with seven old ladies and Mike.

Maybe they don't think of themselves as old ladies, although the youngest is at least her mother's age and they all like to give her advice on where to shop for the best fruit and how to clean a tub without scratching the finish and what kind of man is most likely to be loving and compassionate his whole life long. Considering they are all widowed or divorced, Gina finds this advice ludicrous.

Toward Mike, they are respectful, attentive, and even a bit flirtatious. He takes it all in stride; smiling and impersonal even as he puts his arm around their waists to demonstrate a self-defense move they should use if ever approached in a dark, echoing parking deck

103

after eleven p.m. when all good people should have gone home to bed. Mrs. McKechnie says, "Let somebody try it, just let them try. I'll put their lights out," and she brandishes her cane with ferocious abandon. She lives alone in a ten-room apartment with her arthritic dog. "I'm not afraid!"

"You should be," Mike says. "Fear is your friend. It tells you everything you need to know in order to read a situation." Gina wonders what happens if she *wants* to be afraid? "Remember," Mike adds, "not everyone wishes you well and your enemies are not always strangers." He smiles and pats Mrs. McKechnie's shoulder reassuringly – and suddenly her cane is twenty feet away, sliding across the brown and gold linoleum and all their breathing stops in their chests as they see her drop to her knees under Mike's grip. Or, almost to her knees. Before she can hit the floor, he has caught her around the waist and, smiling, set her on the faded couch with the worn afghan. "See how quickly it can happen?"

They team up in pairs; Gina with Debbie Ogilvie, a 52-year-old divorcee living on her own for the first time in her life. "I don't know if I can do this," Debbie says as they brace their sneakered feet against each other's and attempt to demonstrate the basic break-hold. "If anyone tried to mug me, I'd probably just wet my pants."

"Or scream." Mike looms up next to Gina's left shoulder, dangerously close. "Either way, you might wreck a rapist's plans." He adjusts Debbie's grip on Gina's upper arm. "Watch out, too, for friendly strangers who just want to 'help' you. Trust no one." His ponytail, dark and curly, slides across his upper back as he turns to see how Myra Blackwell manages the elbow jab. Under the cobalt blue of his shirt, shoulder muscles round up big as grapefruit, straining the cloth. Gina guesses he's around thirty-five years old.

Everyone sits on battered metal folding chairs as he continues his lecture. "Be suspicious of the person who volunteers too many details," he writes on the chalkboard. "They're probably lying. No matter how many reasons they give, never go somewhere with a stranger." He sluices back his hair with one hand and lights a cigarette. They're not supposed to smoke in here, but he ignores that. He's a rule-breaker. The kind of man who sets off alarms - not in buildings, but in women's hearts. Every good girl is fascinated by bad boys.

"Don't let anyone do you a favor, or worse yet, a series of favors," he says, frowning when Kiki Becker whispers to Myra Blackwell. "It's a form of loan-sharking. Eventually they want payment."

Kiki begins to giggle, then raises her hand. "How do you know? Maybe the guy is just flirting, trying to get to know me. Good lord, I haven't had a man spontaneously offer to help me in years. Are you sure you're protecting us, Mike? I can't find a guy that good to *date*, let alone spray Mace on him."

The other women titter and Gina imagines Mike offering to carry her grocery bags up the stairs, to fix that leak in the kitchen. Her cheeks flush when she thinks about how she might repay him. She quivers at the thought of touching his lips, sliding her hands around his waist, pressing her breasts against that muscled chest.

"You have to make choices," he says, concluding the lesson. "Avoid confrontation, be aware of your surroundings and survive. Trust your instincts and realize nothing can be taken for granted."

Class is over until next Tuesday. Mike reminds them to go to their cars in pairs. Gina walks out with Georgia Frye, a heavyset mother of four whose husband was killed last year in a three-car pile-up on the Martin Luther King expressway. Georgia shakes her head as they stand next to her '93 Chevy Cavalier. "All I want is to feel strong, like I can protect my family, you know? I realize there's no such thing, but I'd like to enjoy the illusion." She sits down heavily and a bucket of Legos tips over, a hundred red and white bricks cascading to the floor. With an impatient movement, she kicks them over to the passenger side and shakes her head again. Gina waves good-bye and gets into her own car. Mike stands at the church doorway, lighting another cigarette. He glances up as a dark-haired woman strides by, then zips his jacket and leaves.

Gina starts her car and follows his taillights, her radio tuned to the all-news station. Harrowing accounts of true-life tales. Robberies at gunpoint, assaults, children abducted from their beds. All the scariest things anyone could imagine, and God knows, she has a vivid imagination. It brought her to this city, after all.

The thing she keeps wondering, though, is how far can fear take her? Away from the homogenized, sanitized suburbs, away from her apartment-cocoon, her modular office cubby, saving her life like spaghetti in Tupperware until it congeals and stiffens to inflexible strands. Saving it for what?

Mike heads for the rougher side of town, and she follows, stalking him, afraid to show her face, but more afraid to stay in calm waters all her life. He parks near a ragged strip mall, where a tattoo shop cuddles up to a gym and music escapes through the door of a neighborhood tavern. He comes here every Tuesday night after class and, lately, so does Gina.

But he doesn't see what she sees, from across the parking lot. He doesn't see himself, leaning against the wall outside the gym, waiting until the aerobics instructor leaves. The aerobic instructor is lean and gorgeous, with six-pack abs and a smooth white exercise bra. He's hooked. She always looks him up and down, her gaze disparaging, her silky little moustache twitching when she sees his cigarette and Mike – Mike of the muscular shoulders and macho security-advisor status and small C-shaped scar on the back of his neck – he swallows convulsively, his Adam's apple going berserk. Then she passes him by, an uber-chick in tights, and he throws away his cigarette, standing under the security light alone with the moths until, finally, he gets in his car and drives off.

Be afraid, Mike says, be very afraid. Trust your instincts; save your life. Gina thinks everyone fights fear with fear, striking and recoiling on themselves with words, with weapons, tactics, bargains, tricks and prayers. But what she's mostly afraid of is staying safe in the city, never risking what she might find. So tonight, she's following Mike to his apartment on South Street, walking across his dark parking lot alone, ringing his doorbell, ignoring all seven of the warning signs, and she's not saving her life.

From the Sky

THE FERRY RIDE OVER TO THE ISLAND is slow and windy in winter. I stood at the railing, thinking of nothing, just staring out across the water at the gray on gray horizon. The stiff breeze forced tears from my eyes and dried them off before they could leave more than faint salty tracks on my face. I wore a scarf and my long woolen coat. All my possessions were lined up at my side in battered suitcases and bundles.

Then the baby fell out of the sky and everything changed.

I had no warning. No premonition, no illumination. Just a sudden impending rush, startling me, making me step back, my mittened hands still spread toward the railing. That baby dropped into my arms like Wednesday into Thursday, as easy as that. "It's a baby," I said stupidly. It seemed the only thing to say, but then I'm not quick on the uptake.

She was a cute little baby, wrapped in a pink alphabet-print quilt and smelling faintly like peanut butter. Two slivers of teeth showed through her drooling smile. There came a shout from above and I looked up to see a hot-air balloon traveling silently through the mist. There were people in the basket, not so silent, and one woman in hysterics. I held the baby up for them to see. "She's okay," I called. "See? Everything's fine."

One of the men motioned toward the ferry landing and I nodded, gathering myself together. The baby, her legs pumping, took both hands to carry. One of my bags or bundles, once considered so necessary, would have to be lived without.

Once we were all on shore the people from the balloon thanked me over and over again. "You saved her life!" they cried, and the formerly hysterical woman kissed my cheeks. "It must have been an act of God."

"No, just luck," I said modestly. "Nothing to it." I began to walk away but they stopped me, insisting that I must take some kind of reward. I shook my head.

"Take the baby," the woman suddenly said, pushing her into my arms again. "It's the least I can do. She's yours."

I looked into that little face, the rosebud mouth, the long-lashed eyes. "Thank you," I said. "I have always wanted a baby."

It wasn't easy, carrying that baby and all my things (or most of them, another bundle abandoned) up the hill to the hotel, but I did it. No one will ever know how much work that was. The woman at the registration desk looked at me oddly but I paid no attention to her. A room with a bath was all I needed, some shelter against the impending storm. Was a little privacy too much to ask?

The room, high under the attics, featured a round window looking out on the shore. Waves beat against the rocks, lashed by rain that had begun streaming in on long horizontal streaks. The baby slept. I foraged in my bundles for something to eat – an apple, some rather soggy graham crackers. Someone knocked at my door and a man stood there, a waiter. White apron, black vest, he held a tray with a bottle and glass. "Wine?" he asked.

The wine, rough and red, filled my mouth with longing. "How did you know this was just what I needed?" I asked, leaning back in the rocking chair, crossing one knee over the other.

"I've always known." The waiter had dark curly hair. I had to look a long way up to see his face. The room had become darker and an occasional flash of lightning gave things a strange color. "Would you like to walk?" He held out his hand to me.

The wind whipped the tails of my cloak as we made our way down to the beach. We could barely follow the narrow path between the rocks, edged by white shells, and I had to fight for each breath. The wine had warmed my heart, but my teeth chattered and my hands grew numb. Blinded by rain, I reached out and felt his arm strong and steady beneath my fingers. "I don't want you to leave your wife," I said. "That would be wrong."

"She left me years ago," he replied and held me close. "I've been praying to God I would find someone like you. And now it's happened."

"God has nothing to do with it. This is pure luck." I kissed him and the thrill his lips sent through my body matched the streaks of lightning pounding down around us. A wave caught us by surprise, taking him down, making us stagger and grasp at each other. My cloak was too heavy. I had to get it off before it pulled me under. The clasp wouldn't give and I tugged at it, ripping the fabric in desperation. As I finally fought my way free and crawled up the beach, the waiter waved good-bye.

"It was nice knowing you," he called as the riptide dragged him under. His fingers still clutched my cloak and I knew I'd never see it again. Or him. Probably just as well. He was still married and I would never choose to be the Other Woman.

The restaurant at the hotel was well-lit, noisy and full when I stumbled in, wringing water out of my hair and clothes. Several heads turned and the lady from reception gave me a cold eye. "Boiled eggs," I told the waitress, "and plenty of them." On second thought, I asked her to send the meal up to my room. The restaurant was too bright and I had lost my sunglasses, along with several small maps.

The baby was still sleeping soundly, soundlessly, when I got back. I had surrounded her on the bed with pillows, red and pink, to make sure she couldn't roll off or get washed away. God forbid! As I changed into dry clothes I reflected that, with one thing or another, I was running out of luggage. Pretty soon, I'd have nothing to carry at all. Then, what would I do?

Once, I dreamt of climbing mountains. Maybe if I could reach a mountaintop, close to the heavens, God might reveal his plans. But then again, it might be just my luck to catch him on an off day. Luck is like that; it can be good or bad. Or maybe even God or bad.

Maybe Luck follows people around, drags behind them like toilet paper caught on their shoe, trips them up. Maybe Luck is as simple as a restaurant having boiled eggs when you want them. How long could it take to boil some stupid eggs?! Was I not a paying guest? Did I not deserve the same consideration as anyone else? How long were they going to make me wait?

I found myself standing on the edge of the tub, tugging on my belt, that cotton terry belt, that rope, holding it twisted like fate. What *is* fate? Is it predestination or serendipity? Are we meant to have a purpose or are all the bad things that happen to us just the luck of the draw? Is everything simply God's celestial joke? The shower rod was flimsy, not like the solid sturdy rod of my youth, when bathroom fixtures were made to last forever, in calypso turquoise and pink. Perhaps I should never have left home, but remaining was not an option.

The baby began to fuss and I climbed down from the ledge. Responsibility called. Besides, that curtain rod would never have held my weight. She waved her little fists and kicked, making sounds expressive of severe disapproval. Not that I blamed her. There were no instructions within the folds of her swaddling, no directions, no grand exhortations to Do This! Do That!. I'd have to muddle through on my own. "This is what happens, Baby," I crooned, kissing her foot and getting toes up my nose. "I was not prepared. One seldom is when things fall from the sky. Perhaps you'd like a graham cracker?"

Perhaps she would not. I glanced with dismay at the spreading dampness on the totally unsuitable blue satin sheets. Why would anyone put blue satin sheets on a bed with a baby? Oh God, I thought, you sent me a baby from the sky? Couldn't you have thrown in a box of Huggies?

"Don't worry," I sighed as her squawkings grew louder and somewhere a teakettle began to shriek. "This is not what I signed up for but we'll manage. Really! I'll teach you how to play Skip-Bo and we'll grow to love each other."

114

"I don't know about that," the baby replied, shooting me the stink eye. "You can't even get a boiled egg, for God's sake."

Leap Year

If I had an extra day
I could catch up on the ironing
I could clean my linen closet and get the ragged
Towels to the bottom of the pile
Where they belong

With an extra day, I could
Work in the yard, I could
Weed and plant instead of looking
Out the window and always thinking
"I ought…."

If I had an extra day
It wouldn't be a Monday
Because Mondays are self-righteous and cold
And it wouldn't be a Friday
Because Fridays are lazy and ne'er-do-well

I think it would have to be mid-week,

This extra day, and in the autumn
When the air is fresh and the sky
Becomes a Spanish tile of blue and white
Suspended overhead.

I'd rise early, this day not to waste.
My coffee would be freshly ground and
I'd drink it outdoors, listen to the breeze
And share my muffin with a robin
Or a wren.

On my extra day, I'd drive by the steam plant,
Whose triple towers send billowing clouds
I wouldn't have to crane my neck and keep
One eye on traffic. I'd just park my car
And watch them rise.

On this special day, I'd visit my parents
And take flowers to their graves. I'd sit
On the cemetery bench and talk with my brother
And I'd remember how they lived
And not how they died

On this extra day, this bonus, this *lagniappe*,
I'd tell my loved ones how rich they make me feel
How, surrounded by them, I am rich enough,
Wealthy enough, to not really need
This extra day.

Something to Talk About

IN ALMOST ANY BOOK OR ARTICLE you read about strong, long-lasting relationships, good communication is described as vital. *Talk* to each other, these articles admonish. Most married couples spend only seventeen minutes a day talking to each other. It's not enough.

Well, I say, talk is cheap.

My husband and I talk to each other. And our marital shorthand is so good, we can sometimes complete our daily allotment in fifteen minutes or less. "Did you remember to…?", he asks, and I say "Yes," saving us from the necessity for further discussion or the rudeness of pointing.

I mean, what is there to talk about anyway? Politics? Yikes. Religion? God forbid. The current state of our finances? Don't even go there. I already know my husband's position on furniture-moving, the best route to Circuit City, and how, precisely, the Hurricanes failed to win the Stanley Cup. He is aware of my views on radio deejays, pet hamsters, and vicious editors who refuse to respond to manuscript submissions in a timely

118

manner. We really don't need to spend any more time talking about these subjects and, in fact, could probably quote large swathes of our mate's previous discourses from memory.

Besides, talking is only half the equation. The other part is listening, and there's the rub. We assume we know what the other person is saying, and why, and usually we're right. When my husband wanders into the kitchen on a Sunday evening and stares into the fridge, asking me questions like "How old is that ham?", I just smile and go about my business. I know if I leave him alone, he'll work his way through the leftovers and maybe even clean out the vegetable bin for me. Likewise, when I come home from an afternoon with my mother, he knows it's okay to sit at the kitchen table, reading his paper and occasionally nodding, while I rant. I'm just going through the emotional equivalent of cleaning out the fridge and, in fact, if he were to offer insight at that moment, I'd probably shove his head into the Crisp'n'Cold.

Sometimes I think that facial expressions and a carefully-crafted form of sign language would be best. Something along the lines of baseball signals. For example, when he wants to know why there are no clean socks in his drawer, he could hold out his foot and waggle the toes. I could then respond with a wink and a one-fingered point at the laundry room. Or if I wish to comment on his choice of a tie, I could merely grab my neck with one hand, and my nose with the other, all the while vigorously shaking my head. He could tell me how his day at work had gone by merely slamming his briefcase across the dining room table and I could moan about the kids by banging my head against the wall until I passed out. Oh, wait, I forgot. We already do that.

The fact is, after being married for a quarter of an eon, we already know so much about each other that we think we know it all. It's easy to miss the signs that something new is going on. Or maybe we really don't want know. If he's not feeling well, I need be aware of that, but I don't want to talk about it. He's supposed to stay young and strong forever. I know that people age and grow old and sometimes develop health problems, but talking might make it real. Might make it happen to *us.* So I listen with half an ear, my motor running, trying to think about other things, safer things, things over which I have control.

Or sometimes we talk but in a surface-y way. We express our wonder at stuff in the news - bombs, murders, priests who prey on children. We comment on what those people should do or not do or how they should have acted, but we don't say, "Hey - what's happening? Where are we going? How scary is this? How could such a thing be?" because it's too terrifying. The truths are too real. We'd rather keep them at arm's length. Are we headed to war? Is a mother who kills her kids crazy or evil? Could it be possible there's really no God at all? The possibilities that could be opened up are horrifying, like finding out that gravity doesn't really exist and we only keep our precarious toehold on earth by pretending to believe. What do you hold onto? Where is your foundation?

Add to these problems the difficult questions of where and when. Can't talk with my husband right after work, when I'm running around trying to slap dinner on the table and he's wolfing down a banana, fighting the irritability that goes with low blood sugar. Can't talk with him after dinner when the news is on and children are coming to us with petty arguments and pressing problems in math. Can't talk in the car when we're stuck in gridlock and a simple comment about how someone (I won't say who) never puts toilet paper back on the roller quickly becomes a full-blown rant about the mega-ton overload of junk in our house.

Methinks the best form of communication is physical. John Lennon said "Love is touch, Touch is love." He's right. The first thing we seek as newborn infants is our parents' touch. Their warm arms, the beat of their hearts. As children, when we're weary or upset, we crawl into our mother's lap or hang onto daddy's shoulder. As teenagers, we become surly, pull away from our parents' touch, but we also begin to look at others, drawn toward a new kiss, a hug.

So for adults, at night, we have this time when we can communicate. Just let go of the day's worries, like dropping a heavy bookbag off our backs, climb into bed and turn on our sides, spooning against each other in the fetal curl of coupling. His arm around me, his lips against the back of my neck. That's when I know how much we still need each other, how we look to each other for comfort and strength against all the crap in the world. After the workday drain and the traffic jams and the spilled milk of our lives, we can turn to each other and say whatever needs to be said, without a single word. If you think sex is important in the early stages of a relationship, just wait. It can take on whole new layers of meaning as the years go by and I'm convinced that couples who play together, stay together.

I dunno. It'd be a lie if I said my husband and I don't need to talk. We do. We need that deep connection which is the only thing that makes marriage worthwhile. It's not easy living day after day with the same person, year after year, through arguments and differences of opinion and plain old fights. I want someone who knows me well, who understands me even when I can't find the words to say what I mean. And I want to know him, to understand how he feels about his choices in life. I want to be there to cheer him on and build him up and let him know there's at least one person in this world who thinks he's a hell of a guy.

All I'm saying is that talk is cheap. You can cover the who, what, where, and when. You can discuss and plan and exchange ideas till the cows come home, but don't forget the why and how. My husband and I communicate because we want to be one, to be so close there's no way that anything this world throws can separate us. And we try to remember, communication is not just the words that are said. With every movement, every gesture, every touch of our hands, we can choose to say *I love you* or *I don't care*. In a long-term relationship, it's entirely possible to talk less and still say a whole lot more.

Then again, maybe this is something he and I should talk about.

The Warm Curve of the Throat

AUNT JODY'S APARTMENT IS AS NEAT as a pin. I didn't expect that. I'm not sure what I did expect; changes, I guess. Something exotic maybe, with velvet curtains and swag lamps and clothes strewn around, something that perhaps whispered *sin* and a thumbing of the nose to the rules that the rest of us live by. At the very least I expected dirty dishes and overflowing ashtrays.

Instead there are flowered curtains and cheerful blue place mats and sunshine coming through the window so that the whole place looks like an advertisement in the Penneys catalog. Aunt Jody tosses her car keys onto the counter and carries my duffel bag down the hall and I follow obediently, caught in her draft like a scrap of paper, stepping suddenly into a small room with wood paneling and plaid upholstery. A guy's room, a masculine room, so surprising that it hits me in the face like a pair of gym socks.

"This opens up to a bed," she informs me, waving her hand at the couch. There are sports posters on the walls—the Charlotte Bobcats, Kyle Petty, the Carolina Panthers. A big screen TV monopolizes one wall. Uncle Kendall must have had it pretty good, I think. His very own room for watching sports, all that man stuff, and Aunt Jody in the kitchen, cooking him man-foods like chili or gumbo, rich and spicy, and I wonder why he ever left. And why Aunt Jody has never changed this room in three years.

I sit on the edge of the couch and I guess I must look kind of nervous because Aunt Jody sits down next to me and gives me a hug.

"It's all going to be all right, baby," she says, whispering into my ear and making it tickle, her perfume so sweet and warm that I want to just curl right up into her, curl up and be the baby, but I don't because I'm not the baby and it just wouldn't be right. Besides, I'm a good five inches taller than Aunt Jody and my elbows and knees are always poking out where they shouldn't. I'm not sure if I can even curl up into a ball any more. When you're a 14-year-old girl who's already five feet, nine inches tall and still growing, people expect you to act your age. Or even older.

"Come on," she says, pulling me to my feet and giving me a little slap where I sit down. "We're going to cook your daddy the best dinner he ever ate. I've got some pot roast and potatoes, he's going to think he died and went to heaven."

"He's not my daddy," I remind her, and she looks at me. No. He's not *my* daddy at all.

*****

It's fun, sitting in Aunt Jody's bright kitchen, watching her cook. You can tell she is really enjoying having someone to cook for. She's got the radio turned on and is dancing a bit, swinging her hips, singing lyrics, ditty-bopping along. She wears an apron, one of those striped canvas jobbies with the patch pockets and bib. I sit on a high stool, peeling potatoes badly. Thick white hunks of the potatoes are going down the drain along with the peel, but she doesn't seem to care. I cut out the bad spots and eyes with the end of the peeler, twisting the sharp metal and leaving deep pockets in the white flesh, running the whole thing under cold water and then casually setting it aside and reaching for the next one. Aunt Jody cuts up carrots, arranging them around the roast, sprinkles the meat with herbs. I try to imagine her naked. She has a pretty good figure for someone her age, but nothing that would really knock your socks off. I mean, she just looks normal. She has little freckles on her nose and sort of wide square teeth that make her smile seem even bigger than it is, and she really doesn't look any different from any other woman.

126

I've never actually *seen* the pictures. I think Mumma has a copy of the magazine but she never has let me look at it. Not even when it first came out and there was all that hullabaloo and Grandma saying she could never hold her head up in town and Mumma going around with her lips pressed tight shut. They never let me in on anything anyway. I'm the village idiot.

In fact, I'm surprised I'm even here, in this den of iniquity as Grandma would say, and I suppose it's only because Grandma has her hands full with Grandpa these days that they let me stay here at all. She probably thinks Aunt Jody would do something to corrupt me, like introduce me to Hugh Hefner or something. Ha, as if.

The pot roast goes into the oven and Aunt Jody hands me some plates and tells me to set the table. Brian will be here soon, after spending some time at the hospital with Mumma, and so I set three places, shining white plates on the blue place mats, plates with little flowers in yellow and blue, silverware, glasses. I fold paper napkins into triangles and set them under the forks, just like Mumma does for Thanksgiving dinner. It almost seems like a celebration but it's not. Mumma is not going to be here, she'll have some yucky old soup or something on a tray in the hospital bed and someone will have to feed it to her.

Lying down flat on her back like that, probably half of it will run down her neck, down onto the pillowcase, making it cold and wet against her, not a celebration at all. And Aunt Jody and Brian and I will be here, in this bright kitchen, eating this meal that she has been so happy to prepare, and all of us trying to have conversation, trying to be polite and get past the strangeness. I wonder if Brian will be looking at Aunt Jody, wondering what she looks like naked. Maybe he knows. Maybe he's already seen the magazine, Miss September, nearly three years ago. Maybe at night when Mumma's asleep, he gets quietly out of bed, opens a drawer, feels around under nightgowns and slips to find it, takes it into the bathroom, opens it up and looks at Aunt Jody naked. I hate him, and all men, for wanting to look and I hate Aunt Jody for letting them.

Bile comes up in my throat and I swallow it down, force it back where it belongs. I drink some cold water. Aunt Jody looks at me and frowns. Does she know what I'm thinking?

"You okay, baby?" she asks, feeling my forehead. "You're white as a sheet."

I'm okay, I tell her. I don't want her touching me. I feel warm under my skin and I'm sure there are sweat beads where my hair grows from the top of my forehead, making it twist into those tiny, telltale curls.

There's a banging at the door and Brian comes in. He looks tired and fussed and Aunt Jody is fluttering around him like he's Billy Graham, come to give us The Word.

"She's still doing all right," he reports, "The doctor says probably in the morning. She's coming along fine and everything looks good." She, he says. As if he were talking about just anyone, just any woman who is flat on her back in the hospital, waiting to have a baby, any woman who is foolish enough to get pregnant at the age of 36, any woman who might or might not have complications and bleeding and spasms of pain. Aunt Jody fusses over him, offers him a drink, takes his jacket and hangs it up. I'm disgusted with them both.

*****

The pillow is cool when I turn it over and I press my face into it, try to make the blank white of the pillowcase merge with my brain, blot out the dreams and images that are contorting my thoughts, twisting my guts. I lay completely flat on my stomach, pressed to the lumpy mattress of the foldaway. From toes to knees, from pubic bone to ribs, flat as can be. It's no good, I can't rest and I get up and go to the bathroom. The overhead light hurts my eyes and I lean close to the mirror, watch my pupils contract, cover my eyes with my hands until they get used to darkness and then stare some more into the mirror, watching my pupils contract again. When I have tired of this, I take the hairbrush and start brushing my hair. I bend at the waist and brush upside down so that when I stand straight, my hair falls lushly, full and wantonly. I look decades older, I'm sure. I lift my chin so that my cheekbones come into prominence, stare at my eyes to see how knowing they become. I bring my hands up under my T-shirt, cupping my breasts, giving myself a fuller shape. I imagine a man looking at me, being seduced by my beauty, wanting me. I lick my lips and smile a little. Then I blow a raspberry at myself and go back to bed.

*****

Aunt Jody and I sit in the waiting room. It's ugly, full of tan furniture and old magazines. Aunt Jody is flipping through a *People* magazine, reading bits of it out loud to me. I have my Walkman with me, earplugs in, listening to Nickelback. Brian, of course, is allowed in with Mumma.

"I don't want you to think badly of Aunt Jody," Mumma said once, just once after the news came out about the centerfold. "She's not really that kind of person. I think she has been a little mixed up ever since Uncle Kendall left." She said this to me after we'd been at Grandma's house, after Grandma and Aunt Jody had a screaming argument and Grandma offered Aunt Jody a knife to cut out her heart, just cut it out since she'd already done it anyway and Aunt Jody said that for

130

once, just for once, Grandma should consider that maybe not everything had to do with her and that it was nobody else's business what Aunt Jody did but that she'd made a boodle of money out of the deal so everyone else could jolly well take a flying leap. Oh, yeah.

It was kind of exciting there for a minute, but like always whenever anything interesting happens, they scooted me out of the room. I had to go out in the garden while people were screaming at each other and throwing things right there in Grandma's kitchen with the pictures of Jesus curing the Leper on the wall. And Grandpa yelling at them all to quit squalling because he was trying to watch his fishing show and for heaven's sake, they'd all always known Jody was no good, any woman who'd work as a bartender, after all. And them good Baptists, too.

Mumma may not have wanted me to think badly of Aunt Jody but I noticed that they didn't spend so much time together after that. I haven't even seen Aunt Jody more than a couple of times since then. "Some things are hard to explain," Mumma says.

And now Mumma is in the delivery room. Mumma with her modesty and her blushes, laying splayed open to everyone's view, offering up her naked self to the doctors and nurses and anesthesiologist and especially to Brian, so that his baby could be born. I try to imagine it, imagine her laying there with her legs spread wide, self-consciousness gone with the wind, her big belly rolling and quivering as she tries to push that baby out of her body. I can picture her body, white and smooth, straining and working, but I can't picture her face. She's gone somewhere, her face is far away; her mind, her thoughts, her feelings, they're far from this scene of sweat and blood and physical sensation. I can't imagine my mother even being in the same room with her own naked body. Let alone Brian's.

Tears suddenly spurt from my eyes and nose and mouth. I know I'm losing her, know that the separation is complete. Before Brian came along, she was mine, my mother. We could argue and yell at each other but at the end of the day, I could crawl into her lap and know that that space belonged to me. I had claim to the sweet smell of her, that warm spot in the curve of her throat. We were enough for each other.

Aunt Jody is there. With Kleenex and murmurings, she takes me into the Ladies' Room and I cry hard into the sink, bawl like a spoiled toddler, rub my fists into my eyes. Snot runs from my nose like a river and Aunt Jody keeps pushing tissues into my hand. Finally I stop. My hair is sticking up like dried grass and my face is blotchy and red. I'm a mess. Aunt Jody puts her arms around me and rocks back and forth, crooning gently. I feel like I tower over her, all awkwardness and elbows. I just want to go home. She takes me back to the waiting room. A large and noisy family has come in, they are in high good humor. The father is fat and going bald, he holds a dirty-faced little boy in his arms, two girls sit on the floor and play with Barbie dolls. "Pretty soon," he keeps saying, "pretty soon we'll have the new Baaaaaaby."

Brian comes out of the delivery room. He's wearing a smock of yellow paper over his clothes, yellow paper booties on his feet, yellow paper shower-cap over his hair, yellow paper mask dangling below his idiot grin. His very eyeglasses gleam.

"It's a girl!" he crows, giving Aunt Jody a hug. He goes to hug me and I step back. He loses his smile for a minute and then hugs me, hard, anyway. "Your Mom is doing great," he whispers in my ear, holding my head in both his hands, "She says to tell you she loves you." I stand there, breathing hard. If he doesn't stop it's going to make my nose start dripping again.

He lets go just in time and tells Aunt Jody that she should take me home for a little while and we can see Mumma later. I want to see her right away but he says she needs her rest and I can come in about an hour. I don't want him to tell me this; she's my mom. I want to see her. Let *him* go wait an hour. But Aunt Jody is pulling my arm, and I stumble after her, weakling that I am.

All the way home in the car, Aunt Jody is just chattering away, going on and on about how wonderful it will be, having a baby in the family again. She makes me think of the sound squirrels make when you chase them away from the bird feeder and I rest my hot face against the cold car window. My skin sticks to it and I peel away from time to time to find a new cool spot. I want to peel my whole face away, a bit at a time, but it proves impossible to work around the angles of my nose so I give up. I feel tired to death.

It doesn't seem right to just sit in the kitchen and drink coke and eat potato chips after a day like this. Aunt Jody putters around, taking meat out to defrost and washing vegetables. She has a smile on her face the whole time, like she just won the publishers' clearinghouse sweepstakes, like there's something just *wonderful* about all these changes. She makes me sick and I want to punch her in the gut.

"Did you enjoy posing naked?" I ask her, the words like shards of glass. I should be ashamed, I guess, but it was worth it to wipe that smile off her face. She looks down at the counter for a minute and then at me.

"Would you like to see it?" she asks. She knows I never have. I don't know how she knows, but she does. I think this is what they mean when they say someone's called your bluff.

"Uh, no, don't think so," I say and make a disgusted expression.

Her face goes completely blank, *click*, like that, like someone just shut off a light, and she goes to the pantry closet. From the back, she pulls out the

134

magazine. I've seen girly magazines before, behind the counter at the convenience stores, and once at someone's house where I was babysitting, but I've never seen this one, this particular one.

She sets it on the table in front of me and turns the pages. She's standing behind me, bending over me, one hand on the back of my chair, the other turning those pages. When she gets to the right one, she straightens up, her shadow falls away from the picture. I can feel the flush rising in my cheeks, the warmth of embarrassment coming over me. I know I've pissed her off.

In a way, the pictures are beautiful. Aunt Jody doesn't really look like herself, she has all this makeup on and her hair is fixed differently. I can't stop looking at her skin. It's like velvet with a shine and she smiles right into the camera, all soft and welcoming. I don't see how any man looking at her can keep from falling in love with her, plop, helplessly, hopelessly, forever.

"Aunt Jody, you're beautiful," I whisper. She really is. It could break your heart. She reaches over and takes my hand.

"It was something I had to do just then," she says, and then closes the magazine and puts it away. She shuts the closet door and turns to face me and she's regular old Aunt Jody again, with the freckles and Mumma's eyes and Grandma's hands. She reaches out and runs her fingertips along my face, over the curve of my cheekbone and jaw. "I never meant to hurt your grandma and your mom. I can't explain it."

*****

Mumma's hospital room has blue wallpaper with little girls and boys in brown, dressed in old-fashioned clothes and running along, rolling hoops with sticks. Mumma is sitting up a little, her hair a wild mat of black against her pillow. In the crook of her arm, wrapped up in a blanket so that I can hardly see it, is the baby. Kinsey. Brian is sitting next to the bed, practically half-lying on it, his arm around Mumma's pillow, while she smiles and gestures to me to come closer. There's a strained feeling in the air as Grandma and Aunt Jody try to pretend there's no problem between them. Aunt Jody has a big basket of flowers and she's fussing around, trying to fix up the room so it looks pretty, and Grandma busies herself folding and refolding the baby's little bitty clothes. I stand there, arms and legs about ten yards long, trying to think of something to say, watching Grandma's long fingers and bright red nails flashing in and out among the miniature pajamas and undershirts. If only everyone would leave and I could climb in bed with Mumma, but they're all watching me, waiting to see if I'm going to throw a jealous fit, so I'm just not going to give them the satisfaction.

Brian moves back, out of the way and I walk over, my feet feeling as big as watermelons in their Nikes, and loom over the bed, trying not to startle anyone with my Zulu-like stature. I want to look at Mumma, drink in the sight of her, but my eyes catch on that little fluff of black hair above the baby blanket and I can't see anything else. It feels different, holding a baby, than I expected. I know to place my arm under her head, to support its weight, but I am surprised by the curve of her butt, the limpness and roundness of her. She seems so loosely put together, each part moving in its own direction, it's like trying to hold a water balloon. I shift her in my arms, trying to keep her gathered up, before she slips away. I sit down in the chair and Brian puts a pillow in my lap to set her on. Her hair is dark and plastered to her little red skull. Her skin is red, too, and wrinkled, her eyes just a pair of folds above and to either side of her nub of a nose. Her mouth seems too large for her face, crushed and folded in on itself. She yawns and stretches and I watch, fascinated by her doing something that every grown person does; she is nonchalant about this first exercise and opens her eyes to look at me. Mumma. She has Mumma's eyes. My eyes. Aunt Jody's eyes.

I press my lips to her cheek; I can't help it. There's something in that velvet softness that requires it and I breathe in her smell, warm and secret, a trace of Mumma's perfume on her, and a bit of hospital cleanliness. I want to bury my face in the folds of her little neck but I'm afraid her head will loll back and everyone will jump and say *Watch It* so I just touch her little fingertips. The nails are surprisingly long and uneven, tiny slivers of nail, scratching at the end of long fingers, Grandma's fingers, and she clutches at me, holding on with all her strength, yet casually, as if she has known all along how it would be.

*****

Later that night, I stretch out on the foldaway at Aunt Jody's house. Here in this very room, Uncle Kendall used to watch football and Nascar races. At some point, he decided that all this, and Aunt Jody to boot, was not enough and he walked away. My Daddy, too, did not feel the need to stay, to hang in there with his wife and his little daughter. Brian seems happy to be married to my mom, but who knows if he will always feel this way. Someday it might not be enough for him either. Or it might be too much. Maybe someday I will be married, will have a man that I think is just right for me and maybe he will be and maybe he won't.

I roll on my side and for a minute, I imagine us all together in bed here. Grandma and Aunt Jody, Mumma and me, and now Kinsey. All lying together, curved into each other like spoons. Our skin, all mixed together, from Grandma's blue-edged wrinkles to

Kinsey's little brand new, fuzzy redness. All velvet and shine and sweet smells. I tuck my face against my shoulder, pressing my lips to warm skin. Some things are hard to explain.

Oral Tradition: *Fussing in the Key of G*

GRANDMA IS FUSSING ABOUT GETTING ready for Camp Meeting this year, even though she has it organized down to the last baked bean and roll of toilet paper. She's been going every year since she was born, 1939, and so I guess she knows what's needed, but she really gets into the whole 'tradition' thing. I'll try to stick in something new, like my Ipod or Gameboy, and she throws a hissy fit. "That's not what Camp Meeting is about," she says, packing her sun tea jar and a bag of lemons. "It's about family, and Jesus, and knowing why the good Lord put us on earth. Now where did you put the Skip-Bo cards?

I find the cards, give them to her and tiptoe away. Grandpa is sleeping in the living room in his wheelchair with all the shades pulled and I lay on the floor in the half-darkness. The wide wood boards are cool, but hard, and I can feel my ribs and hipbones grinding against them. My breasts are coming in at last (or should I say going out?) and they mortify me. Mortify is a good word, I learned it in Ms. Crawford's English class. It means death, as in my breasts embarrass me to death, or my breasts make me want to die, or my breasts are just killing me. All the clothes I own are now divided into two groups: Shirts That Show Too Much Boobage, and Shirts That Don't. Nothing worse than walking into a room and realizing too late that your breasts are pointing at people.

It must be kind of like that for guys when they get an unexpected boner. Boner is a funny word, too, and at first when I heard it, I kept thinking of Banjo, that little cocker spaniel that Grandma used to have. He would wag his stumpy little tail and I liked to grab it and hold on. Underneath the skin and muscle, I could feel his tailbones. But I guess boners aren't exactly like that.

Grandpa wakes up. He does this with no sign of waking, just suddenly his eyes are open. "Where's your Grandma?" he says. "Time for the baseball game." And it is, too. Grandma turns on the TV and they both watch the game. Grandpa falls asleep again during the fourth inning. Grandma watches the whole game, now and then gripping Grandpa's arm when it gets exciting.

When I think about it, I've been going to Camp Meeting every year since I was born, just like Grandma, but fourteen years just isn't the same as sixty-one. She keeps telling me how much it's changed, but when I look at the old pictures she has on her wall, seems exactly the same to me. There's the big arbor in the center of the campground, with the stage and pulpit, the rows of pews. Surrounding the arbor, concentric rings of 'tents', the old tin-roofed wooden shacks that have been falling down and rising again since the 1840's. You can always tell which ones are new by the yellow wood. And, of course, the canteen where all the action is.

In fact, the only changes at all that I can see are the fashions. Short-shorts and pointy eyeglasses in the fifties, halter tops and bell bottoms in the seventies. That, plus our family keeps shrinking. In the photos of when Mumma was a kid, over twenty relatives stood on the porch. Now we're down to seven. That's another thing that makes Grandma fuss. "You'd think people could take two weeks a year to spend with their families," Grandma mutters. "It just ain't right how families get all spread out these days."

"Yeah, but it cuts down on the murder rate," Aunt Jody says, popping her gum and grinning at me. The day we move into our tent, she babysits with Grandpa and Kinsey at the house until everything's settled and then brings them out in the evening, him in his wheelchair, Kinsey in the stroller. It's almost like he and Kinsey are the same age nowadays. They both wear diapers and sleep a lot.

In the evenings, Aunt Jody likes to sit on the swing on the front porch of the tent and say hey to all her old boyfriends when they walk by with their wives. She quit bartending and now she's learning to be a mortician. That's another word a lot like mortified, only it means an embalmer of the dead. "Funeral director, if you don't mind," she says. "It's about a lot more than just laying out corpses, you know. I'm going to really change things, too. None of this depressing organ music. Hey, Dwayne." She smiles slowly, her lips with their shiny peach color sliding back over her square, white teeth. "How y'all doin'?"

Dwayne (or Bill, or Travis, or Eddie) always smiles nervously. Aunt Jody hasn't changed much since the time when she posed for that centerfold and the wives always make angry faces when they see her sitting there in her short shorts and little cotton tops. She has real good legs for a woman over thirty, they're brown as peaches with little golden freckles on the thighs, and she likes to cross them real slow. "For example," she continues saying to me, while her eyes follow Travis (or Eddie, or Bill, or Dwayne) as he goes on down the path, "if a person liked to listen to Elvis Presley when they were alive, why not play Elvis music when they die? I'm not talking about the lively stuff, like "Viva Las Vegas", but you could play "Kentucky Rain", couldn't you?" She stops to wipe some drool off

143

Grandpa's chin. He smiles and looks vaguely at her. "And clothes, too. If a person wasn't the type to wear a suit, why not bury him in a golf shirt?"

"I don't think I'd like to look at dead hairy forearms," Grandma snaps, "and if you're want people to take you seriously as a funeral director, maybe you should button your shirt a little higher. I can see clear to China."

Grandma tries to talk Aunt Jody into taking a day off from learning about extracting bodily fluids. "Why?" Aunt Jody asks. "You know we'll only end up fussing at each other."

"We could talk about things."

"No, Mama. We never talk. We just fuss." Aunt Jody checks her hair in her compact mirror and winks at me. "I'll just come in the evenings, I'm on a low-fuss diet these days."

During the day, Grandma watches over Grandpa and cooks stuff for the canteen. I don't think they could even *have* Camp Meeting if she wasn't there to make hush puppies and fried chicken and 'nanner pudding. I hang out with my friend, Ashley, and help with the younger kids during Bible school. Not that anybody asked me if I minded doing it, somehow it's always just expected that the girls will help. Nobody expects it of the boys, which seems unfair to me. They just hang out at the creek all day long, fishing and sometimes skinny-dipping. One day, Ashley snuck off to watch them. She

144

told me about it later but it made me feel so fussed inside my chest that I said I had to go help Grandma with the snapbeans. I don't want to think about that stuff yet.

Lots of people show up for Little Sunday, the first weekend of Camp Meeting. Mumma and Brian spend the whole weekend and we all go to the arbor to hear the preachers and the singers. The Lighthouse Boys are here again this year, and June McSwain, and the Elizabeth City First Methodist Choir. Of course, what everyone really waits for is Reverend Caswell from Mt. Olivet. He's the Bible-thumpingest preacher we've got around here and there's never any telling who might decide to give up their sinning ways and come to Jesus. Some folks have done it three or four times already.

Ashley and I get permission to sit on one of the end pews, near the back. It's so hot out, everyone's got their paper fans going, and Taylor Witherspoon keeps looking at me a lot. He's one of the few boys taller than me, so that's kinda nice and Ashley keeps nudging me and giggling. Taylor wears glasses and they make him look real smart, and he has this sort of slow grin that just does something to me. After the preaching is over, we go walking with a bunch of others down to Ashley's tent. I get all embarrassed and don't know what to say to him, but he just keeps talking about school and playing the trumpet in marching band, and we sit together on Ashley's swing. When he goes to stand up, he puts his hand on my shoulder first. It makes a little thrill run right down my arm and out at my elbow.

It's hot, really hot, even at night and Grandma lets me sleep on the upstairs porch. It's not much cooler but I like to watch the whole place slowly settle down and go to sleep. Then it's just me and the crickets and moths and the stars. The moon rises right up over the arbor, it's the prettiest sight.

Sometimes the boys will gather, quietly, whispering and passing a cigarette, and walk through the campground. I lay still as can be, my face pressed into the pillow that still smells of Grandma's iron-on starch, and try to hear what they're saying. Boys do fascinate me, I have to admit. They're so different from girls and get to do lots better things. I know all about how girls have more opportunity nowadays, Aunt Jody is always telling me that, but it still seems like boys have more interesting lives. The only thing Aunt Jody ever did interesting was when she posed for that centerfold, and Mumma has never done anything interesting at all. Grandpa helped blast holes in the mountains for roads, and Brian is a volunteer fireman and even stupid Lonnie Sigmon down the road drives a dirtbike in moto-cross races. The most exciting thing I ever did was ride the elephant when the Cole Brothers Circus had their show over at the elementary school. It's not a lot to look back on.

Each night the number of visitors grows. Ashley and I get dressed up in the evening after supper. She put a lot of Sun-In on her hair this summer and it really looks good. Mine is all curly from the humidity, so all I can do is stick it up in a big bushy ponytail. I finally got Mumma to let me wear mascara, though, so we both look lots older than last year. We walk round and round the campground, over and over, smiling at the boys and looking to see if they're smiling at us. Friday night before Big Sunday, the crowds are really big. Grandma has been cooking all day at the canteen. "It's too much," Mumma fusses at her. "You can't work all day in that hot kitchen, they shouldn't ask it." Grandma's mouth makes a real straight line and she begins folding napkins and stomps around, putting the silverware straight. Mumma sighs and sits by Brian, who's pushing Kinsey back and forth in the stroller. Brian is always a little nervous around Grandma. He offers her a chair, saying how hot it is and doesn't she want to sit down.

"No, Brian, I'm fine. Didn't you just hear me say I'm fine?"

"Yes, Miz Abernathy, but . . ."

"Then don't be a horse's patootie."

"No, Miz Abernathy," he sighs, running a finger around his collar. I almost feel sorry for him.

Grandpa sits in his wheelchair. Lots of people come by to say hey and Grandma sits next to him, her eyes sparkling. She talks and laughs and pats Grandpa's hand. He smiles and taps his toe to the country music playing on the radio. Every time somebody new walks up, she tells him in his ear who it is. "The Sherrills," she says. "You remember, Junior and Kat."

"Junior and Kat," he repeats, nodding and smiling. He enjoys the homemade strawberry ice cream. Grandma spoons it carefully into his mouth and kisses him on the cheek. "Jenny?" he says loudly. "Jenny. Jenny?"

"I'm right here, Frank."

"Jenny! Where's Jenny?" he says loudly, and people across the way turn to look.

"Time to turn in," Jody says, and undoes the lock on his chair wheels. "Mama, he gets worse every day, you've got to start giving some serious thought. . ."

"When I want your opinion, I'll ask for it, missy."

"No, Jody's right," Mumma insists. "You have to face facts, Mama, you're not as young as you used to be and Daddy's a lot of work. You can't keep on lifting him and bathing him, you're going to hurt yourself one of these days…"

"Well, I'll be dipped in crumbs and fried in hell before I'll let one of my daughters tell me what I can and cannot do!" Grandma's eyes are blazing and her short, curly hair seems to be standing up on her head. I can see the glare of the setting sun behind it outlining her skull. "We get along just fine, Frank and I, and if I need help with him, I have plenty of friends who'd be

148

glad to give a hand. *Glad* to. Don't you be worrying about us. Y'all just go back to your air-conditioned offices and busy, busy lives and let us take care of ourselves." She glares at Mumma and walks over to Grandpa, putting her hand on his shoulder.

"Jenny?" he says. "Don't fuss. You're always fussing."

In the morning, Grandma is in a bad mood. She said she'd teach me how to fry eggs, but it's not going good. I can't seem to get the knack of cracking the eggs open. "Like this," Grandma says, doing it one-handed into the electric skillet out by the back door. Only this time, the yolk breaks. Usually, she'd just flip it over, cook both sides, and make a fried egg sandwich out of it, but this time she makes a hissing noise with her tongue and tosses it out of the pan and into the grass. I don't know what to do, so I try to pick it up with a paper towel. "Oh, don't mess with it," Grandma says, her voice sharp and tight. I leave it where it is, on the grass next to the path, and later I see a dog run over and eat it. "I just don't know any more," she mutters. "Nothing's what it was." I decide that cereal sounds fine for breakfast. I'm not sure exactly what she's talking about, but I know that there's no dealing with Grandma when she's in one of her moods.

It rains that afternoon. I usually like rain at Camp Meeting. Other years, Grandma and I would sit in the upper room and play cards. Little puffs of rain-cooled air would slip in between the open slats of the wood walls while her hands shuffled the cards, red fingernails flashing. I like thinking about her being fourteen once, and playing cards with her grandma during a warm July rain. "Gin," Grandma would say, and slap down a fan of cards.

But this time she's fussing something terrible. Grandpa's getting heat rash on his - well, under his diaper - and Aunt Jody decides to take him home with her to stay in the air-conditioning. Grandma's so mad she could spit and I decide to go for a walk with Taylor.

Under the pine trees, it's hardly wet at all. Our shoes squelch a little bit on the red mud. Taylor holds my hand. I hope he thinks they're wet from the rain and not from sweat, because all of a sudden I'm nervous. I've been thinking about Taylor just about every minute since he touched my shoulder and worrying that maybe Reverend Caswell is right about the lusts of the flesh. Mine is all goose-bumpy and when Taylor leans down to give me a kiss, I just about die. His lips are soft. They're warmer than I could imagine, making a terrible throbbing start up in my own and I want to lean into him something fierce. Then all at once, I start to shiver all over and we each step back. Gosh, I think, what do I say now - kiss me some more? Instead we hold hands again and walk to the canteen. My hair is getting all frizzed up with the rain but I don't care. Taylor kissed me.

That night it's even hotter and we can hear thunder rolling up from the lake. It's gonna be a whopper of a storm, so Grandma and I take quilts and pillows and a flashlight to the upper room, close under the tin roof. Grandma brings a jug of lemonade and some cookies, too. We nestle in the back seat, reading stuff from the National Enquirer to each other. I like the ones with pictures of celebrity fashions, especially the ones showing the best-dressed and the worst-dressed. "You'd think they could do better," Grandma says, "with all the money they make. Look at that tacky dress. They had style, in my day."

The rain begins really coming down, just about deafening us as it drums on the roof. Grandma's perfume seems stronger up here. Avon's Topaz, which she has always worn till I can't think of anyone but her when I smell it.

"Grandpa had a good afternoon, didn't he," she says, more of a statement than a question. I think about how it seems like he has no chest anymore, he is so curled over on himself. "I wish he could have stayed longer, he'd have liked the singing, I think."

For once she's not fussing. I roll over on my back with my head in her lap and my knees pulled up. "You met him here, didn't you?" I ask. I've heard the story a thousand times, but I have to get Taylor out of my head.

"He was visiting the Hendersons," Grandma says, her eyes closed. "He was just out of the service, almost 30 years old. I was only eighteen. He'd never seen a Camp Meeting before and they had to explain to him about why the cabins are called tents and suchlike. I was working at the canteen and he told Carl Henderson he'd never seen a woman with such a flat backside. I overheard him and said, quick as a shot, 'that's because I don't waste time the good Lord gave me just sitting on it'. He told me later it was what decided him to get to know me better. That I could give him a setdown like that without missing a beat." She strokes my hair for a while and I listen to the rain now drumming soft and steady. "We were married before Christmas." Lightning flashes and I can see Grandma's red lipstick looking dark against her white skin. I roll on my side and mush my face into her stomach. The housedress she's wearing smells like sunshine and warm breezes. "He was so good-looking," she says. "I thought he hung the moon."

She looks down at me, sternly. "Always set your standards high, Jayelle. Don't date any stupid boys, you hear?"

I nod against her warm belly. "Yes, ma'am. I mean, no, ma'am. I mean, I won't."

"Your grandpa was a self-educated man, an intelligent man. He read everything he could get his hands on." After a minute, she corrects herself. "*Is* a self-educated man." Lightning flashes again, with thunder right on top of it and we both jump. "Mercy," she laughs. "Good thing old Banjo isn't here, remember how afraid he used to be of storms? Used to whine and fuss until one of us would go sit with him in a dark closet."

"I miss Banjo. He was a good ol' dog." I loop my first finger around Grandma's belt, tug at it a little. "I felt bad when he got old, he got so shaky and nervous. He shrank down to nothing." I twine my other fingers in Grandma's belt, too, taking hold. "Just like Grandpa," I whisper. "He's disappearing bit by bit, like Banjo did."

"Not quite like Banjo," Grandma says, her voice quiet and tired-sounding. "Banjo just wanted comforting when he got sick. You didn't need to worry about leaving him his dignity. You didn't need to . . ." She hushes up suddenly and looks out the window. Thunder booms real close by and the car shakes with it. She strokes my hair again. "Everything's changing," she murmurs. "I hate it for him."

The storm stops. As if it had wanted to go out with a bang, like 4th of July fireworks, it pounds out a final volley of thunder and lightning and then goes quietly away. Grandma and I go downstairs to the porch for some fresh air. Rain drips from the trees. Even though

153

it's after midnight, lots of people are awake, talking and excited from the storm. Grandma picks up her pot of geraniums that had tipped over and presses the earth back down around their roots. "You'll be fine," she tells them. "Sun'll be back tomorrow."

Big Sunday brings the biggest crowds of all. Everyone dressed up in church clothes and carrying picnic lunches. Grandma goes all out, with slow-cooked barbecue, fresh-made slaw, silver queen corn on the cob. She doesn't have any truck with people who take the easy way out, bringing in tubs of KFC or cardboard boxes from the supermarket deli. "I just don't understand how people can let all their traditions die out." She puts her best tablecloth on the big rough table that Grandpa built in the downstairs room a long time ago, and sets out real plates, not paper ones that can be thrown away afterward. Mumma has made lemon chess pies and Jody puts a jug of daisies in the middle of the table. Grandpa is asleep in his wheelchair, but he wakes up when we're ready to eat. He still likes to eat Grandma's cooking, even if we have to cut it up real small. I take Kinsey out of the stroller. She's cutting teeth now and drools all over my good blouse. When she grins, all that spit makes a bubble. Brian takes her on his knee and we all hold hands to say grace. Grandma adds at the end, "Lord, let us have many more times at Camp Meeting, if it is Your will, Amen." She tucks a napkin under Grandpa's chin.

Everyone begins passing food around. Out of the corner of my eye, I see Taylor Witherspoon sauntering past and looking to see if I'm looking at him. I *am* looking at him, and that throbbing in my lip starts up all over again. Nobody seems to notice. Mumma and Jody are giggling over some private joke, Brian's feeding the baby. From the next tent, we can hear music. Elvis Presley, singing *The Wonder of You*.

"That'd be a good song to use, don't you think? I'm gonna make a list."

"Miz Abernathy, did you hear that the Baptists are debating about whether to use cushions on the pews now?"

"People are too soft nowadays."

"Yes, ma'am. Well, maybe if they were softer, they wouldn't *need* cushions, heh heh."

"Pass me more of that slaw. It's awful good."

"Honey, who's that boy out there? He keeps looking over."

"Anyone want some cornbread? It's fresh made."

"Jenny? Where's Jenny?"

"Right here, Frank."

*****

Note: *Rock Springs Campground, in North Carolina, is the oldest existing site in the U.S. for annual religious Camp Meetings. For two weeks every summer, people meet for worship, singing, socializing and family reunions. The site consists of a large open-air arbor with pews, stage and pulpit, surrounded by concentric rings of hundreds of 'tents'; actually unpainted two-story structures with tin roofs and open-slatted wood walls. The term 'tents' goes back to the first year (1829) when people actually did arrive via horse and wagon and set up in tents. The camp meetings have continued annually since then, with the only exceptions being one year during the Civil War when Union troops were in the neighborhood and in 1948 when there was a polio epidemic. Twice the campground has been decimated by fire. In 1898, it was rudely disturbed by an earthquake, weakening the foundations of many tents and somewhat disturbing the tenters' faith in prayer.*

Flags Waving

HOLD YOUR HEAD HIGH. THAT'S THE VERY first thing they teach in Color Guard. Hold your head high, stay in time with the other girls, and toss that flag for all you're worth. If you've done it right, the flag pole will drop right back into your hands, like it's part of you. And if it doesn't, well, you are still holding your head high.

I see him as we round the corner of Main and Beaufort, halfway through the parade, just as I do the overhead horizontal spin. Dad. Same blonde hair, same square jaw, same way of standing - one hand in a back pocket, the other holding a drink. My hands keep working that flag even though my fingertips buzz. Left, out, swing right. Up, hold, roll out.

He's in front of the bridal shop and just as I pass him, it's flag loop, eyes right and we stare at each other, face to face. Can't tell if he recognizes me, I'm wearing those fake Ray-Bans, but his cup stops halfway to his lips. It's like a tunnel of pure vision between him and me, everything else a blur, and then he's gone, left behind in the crowd as the band swings into *God Bless the U.S.A.*

In front of me, Emily Sigmon drops her flag during the may-spin. I step right over it and keep marching, making sure my feet don't catch on the glittery red fabric. Never stop to pick up a fallen flag because the band marches on. Tilt up, forward, tip left and roll. Drop-spin, butterfly, crazy eight, snap. Left, right, left, right, Dad, Dad, Dad.

Lord a'mighty, it's hot out. Seems like with a hundred years of Old Soldier's Parade tradition, someone should've figured out that August isn't the best time of year for marching in the sun. We get twenty seconds of blessed shade beneath the oaks in front of the library and I see Mumma with Brian and the baby. I wonder if she knows Dad's here. Windmills, front and back, two, three, four.

The parade ends at the bank parking lot. It's full of convertibles with poster-board signs. "Harry Needham, Mayor!", "Rose McKay, Register of Deeds!", "Misty Brunette, Tiny Miss All-American Sweetheart!". The 4H Club climbs off hay bales on the back of Kyle Treadmore's pick-up truck and someone presses a cold can of Sundrop into my hand.

I have to get out of there. Everyone around me is talking but all I can hear is the rattle of my breathing

158

and the roar of my heart. Emily Sigmon is crying and all the girls tell her it's okay, could happen to anyone, but my mind is five blocks back on Main Street. I roll up my flag, put it on the band van, and run to find him. Three whole years since I last saw Dad.

The crowds are still thick, moving toward the big parking lots by Food Lion and Family Dollar, but I cut across the courthouse lawn and zip through the alley behind Main Street. When I come out by the bridal shop I look everywhere, but he's gone. I can't believe it, like was he never there at all. Then, as I wipe sweat out of my eyes, I see him over by Hoyle's Radiator Specialties and call "Dad!" It's no use, there are too many dads in the crowd so I give another yell. "Jesse Lee Yarborough!"

And he turns. Stops where he is, shades his eyes with his hand and looks to see who called. Gives me a smile. A big smile, a good one. "Well, look at you," he says softly when I get to his side. "All grown up."

"Hey," I say, suddenly shy and Dad hugs me, awkwardly with elbows and shoulders banging. Prickly whiskers brush my cheek and I can smell his aftershave and sweat and a little tang of whiskey-touched lemonade. "Hey," I say again.

He looks the same. His eyes are still as blue. Tanned skin stretches tight across his nose and cheekbones, his eyebrows are bleached almost white, and the sun glints off his blonde hair. *Golden Boy.* Little lines are beginning to show at the corners of his eyes. "I saw you waving your flag," he says. "You looked real fine." He sticks his hands in his jeans pockets and looks around at the crowd. "Huh. This town never changes. Sure brings back a lot of memories."

"I have my driver's permit," I tell him. "Three more months of driving with Mumma and I can get my license." There are no pockets in my green uniform shorts. Nowhere to put my hands. "We've got our first game tomorrow night, against Bunker Hill. You want to come?"

"Is that right? Driving already?" A couple of people walking by say hey and Dad heys them back. "Your mama here?"

"Somewhere. You -- you know she got married again, right?"

"I've been told." He squints up at the sun and then laughs, shaking his head. "Brian, of all guys. Shit."

Shane Gerlitz's dad comes up to talk and so do a couple other guys who recognize Dad from the old days. They're all glad to see him and keep asking why he doesn't come around more. Dad talks about Wilmington and the fishing tournaments he's in and I just stand there, feeling all tall and sweaty, until I see Mumma coming along the sidewalk. Brian's pushing

160

the stroller and he's got perspiration beads in his hair, what's left of it, and his face is sunburned.

Mumma smiles, her gaze shooting off sideways, and gives me a hug. "You did great, J.L.. All the girls looked so nice, I'm real proud of you." She pushes her hair back behind her ear, folds her arms and turns to Dad. "Well, Jesse Lee. How are you?"

He's staring at her like they've got that tunnel vision thing going and then he squats down and speaks to the baby. "Well, who are you? You must be Kinsey. I hear you're a pistol." He gives her his finger to hold and squints up at Mumma. "Hey, Elizabeth. Good to see you." Brian shifts from foot to foot and Dad looks at him, too, nodding. "Brian."

"Jesse Lee." They just stare at each other and I can almost hear the snorting and pawing of hooves. "What brings you back to town?"

"Oh, just passing through." Dad stands up again and looks at me. "Checking up on Jayelle here. That okay with you?" he asks, dropping the half-smile. "She *is* my daughter."

"How long are you staying?" Mumma asks. "Maybe you and J.L. can spend some time together."

"Yeah," Dad says, giving Brian the eye-to-eye again. "That can be arranged."

Aunt Jody and I practice the caber toss out in the back yard where we can see our reflections in the

161

sliding glass doors. "You got to spin it real hard," she says, showing me how it's done. The flag pole goes high in the air, end over end, and drops right into her hands. She grins and shimmies at me. "Still got it."

I try but it goes sideways and clatters to the ground.

"Do it again. Keep your elbows tight and don't lean so far forward. And keep your head up."

The next time, I catch it but just barely and Aunt Jody reminds me to smile. "You get extra points for flash, honey. Always go for flash." She smiles at me, bringing out her dimples and that little sparkle in her eyes. When I try, it looks more like a grimace, like I'm holding back a fart or something. Aunt Jody sighs and says, "Let's try that caber toss again."

Mumma comes out from the kitchen and sits on the picnic bench. "Your dad called. He wants to see you tomorrow."

I head for the house but she tells me he's already hung up. "Why didn't you call me sooner?" I ask, throwing my pole on the ground.

"Because he and I had things to talk about." Mumma moves to find a seat in the shade. With her pale skin, she never could take the sun. Aunt Jody turns on the casette tape with the half-time music and we run through the routine. She knows every move and does them side by side with me, watching ourselves in the glass. Even without a regular flag to wave, she looks ten times better than me - cuter, peppier, with tons more style, and a much better figure. She was Homecoming Queen and Color Guard Captain her senior year and it still shows.

"This is like being in a time warp," Mumma says, her voice sounding far away. "Between Jesse Lee and you, Jody, I feel like I should be back in high school, wearing glasses and playing flute."

"Better go do your homework, then," Aunt Jody grins. She does a may-spin/overhand/caber toss combination and the pole lands smack in her hands. "Yep. Still got it." She winks at me and goes indoors.

Mumma rewinds the cassette. As she messes with the buttons, she says, "About tomorrow. . ."

"Don't worry. I have my clothes all ready. Ironed the sash. Cleaned my shoes. We're going to meet early and do everyone's hair in french braids--"

"No, I mean about getting together with your dad." She looks at me, kind of nervous and uptight, like just before she told me she was marrying Brian. "I don't want you to get your hopes up too high."

I notice there's a tiny little rip in my flag, a place where the hem is coming out. Might need to get that fixed before the show, wouldn't want anything to go wrong. I mess with it, saying "We'll probably just hang out. I mean, I'm not expecting anything big, like him deciding he's gonna move back here or something, but you know, it *could* happen."

She meets my eyes and I can guess perfectly well what she's thinking, but jeez, people do change sometimes. Just because *she* couldn't make him stay. . . But we neither of us say anything and she just turns on the cassette player and I practice again. When it's finally too dark to see my reflection any more, we go in the house and Mumma puts her hand on my shoulder.

"He's not a bad person," she says and I twitch away from her, refusing to meet her gaze. "It's just that sticking around isn't the thing Jesse Lee does best. And sometimes you have to let a person be who they are, instead of who you want them to be."

That night, while everyone's asleep, I go down to the den and find Mumma's high school yearbook on the shelf. I flip through the pages I've looked at a thousand times. Aunt Jody in the Homecoming Court. Mumma dressed in her band uniform, a shadow falling across her face and I wonder if maybe she's always like that, in the dark, thinking the worst of people. A little further on, Dad's picture. *Golden Boy*. That's what the caption says and he's smiling there in his green and gold football jersey, sun gleaming off the helmet on one knee. Jesse Lee Yarborough, quarterback, team captain, Class of '81. State champs, the only team from our town ever to get that far, and he's the one led them there.

Dad and I head out toward Juniper Point. They have the best cheeseburgers in the whole state and he lets me drive. It makes me nervous, steering his truck along these narrow, winding roads. I'm afraid of going off onto the shoulder, feeling the tires drop from the edge of the black-top onto the rutted gravel.

"You're doing okay," Dad says. "Picture your right foot in the middle of the lane, where the exhaust tracks are. Stay centered and you'll be fine. More room for error than you'd think."

My hands are perspiring, they want to stick to the steering wheel. "So what have you been doing lately?" I ask. It sounds dumb, like conversation with a stranger. "Anything besides fishing?"

The windows are rolled down and Dad rests his elbow on the sill, wind lifting the golden hairs on his arm. "Just working at the garage." He seems moody today, and I can smell the booze on his breath. I wonder why he bothered to come see me at all if he's not going to talk. We're out in farm country now, rolling past barns and fields and fat lazy cows.

"Will you come to the game tonight?" The question comes out of me quiet enough, but it makes the silence afterward feel like a big black beast in the truck with us.

Eventually Dad says, "Maybe."

It's not good enough. It's not nearly good enough. At the four-way stop, I put on my right turn signal and wait for a bread truck to go by. "Well I wouldn't want you to go out of your way or nothing. It'll be a good show, we've been practicing for weeks. My first half-time show." He says nothing and I tell myself shut up, shut up, shut up, but the words just fall out of my mouth and roll everywhere like dropped change. "You know everyone would be glad to see you." He laughs, a short laugh like a bark. "Well, they would. And Aunt Jody'll be there, and --"

"Brian. I don't think he'll be so glad to see me. Pull over here." I turn into the parking lot of a bait shop and Dad tells me to wait while he goes inside. He's in there a pretty long time and I just sit there like a fool, sweating right through my t-shirt, and when he comes back, he smells like a beer. "No, I don't think Brian would like to see me at all," he says, as if he never stepped out at all. "Can't say I blame him. If I was Brian, I wouldn't want me sniffing around either." He flaps his hand for me to get going.

My face feels hot. Not just late-August-no-air-conditioning hot, but really really hot. Burning. He's got to have a beer just thinking of Brian? And doesn't give a crap about leaving me melting in the truck? I peel out of the parking lot with a screech of tires and Dad grabs the armrest. "Whoa, kid! Take it easy."

Take it easy, like hell. "If you think it's going to be too much trouble, then just never mind, don't bother to come." We round the top of the hill and head back down, curving to the left. "It's not like I'm gonna die of

166

shock. *And my name's not 'kid'."* The road comes down to the creek bed and turns sharply right. I have to pull hard on the steering wheel and press the brake. Gravel sprays out from under the tires and Dad puts his foot on top of mine and grabs the wheel. We lurch down into a bad rut, the truck almost pitching on its nose, and bounce up again, climbing with all four tires. Even with the jouncing, I can't help noticing the rounded curve of Dad's shoulder in front of me and the acrid smell of his sweat. We come to a stop two feet from a stone wall. My heart is beating so hard it makes my ears thud.

I'm expecting him to yell at me, but Dad just lets out a long blast of air and moves the gearshift to Park. He slides back over into his own seat and after a minute says, real quiet, "Looks like you've inherited more than just my name."

That busts it for me and I jerk the car door open and stumble out, cutting across the field, heading I don't know where until I come up against a split rail fence. My chest feels tight and I'm breathing hard and I swear if he comes near me, I'm gonna smack his face till his whole head spins on his shoulders. But he just sticks his hands in his pockets and comes up to the fence, sitting on it like some cowpoke in a western. All he needs is a hat and something to chew on.

"Sorry," is what he says. "I guess you're pretty sore at me."

167

I sit down on the ground. The grass is dry and stubbly and it scratches my legs. I'm thirsty as hell, and tired and disgusted. "Why *are* you home then? Why bother to stop by at all?"

"Didn't plan to." He looks at me and shrugs. "I don't want to hurt your feelings any worse than I already have, but that's the truth. I was just headed back from a tournament in Hendersonville and the truck started acting up. Eddie Hoyle was working on it so I went over to have a look at the parade. Didn't expect to see you there."

So that was it. Shit. What a fool I am, what an idiot. I stand up and dust off the seat of my pants. "I see. Well, at least I know. Think I'd just as soon go home now." I go back to the car and climb into the passenger seat. Dad looks at me a minute, then gets behind the wheel and turns the truck around to head home. The tires hum on the black top and we go four, five miles in silence.

After a while Dad asks me how I like being in the Color Guard.

"It's the light of my life," I say, real crabby-like. Dad makes the turn onto Tucker's Grove Road and I wonder if this will be the last conversation I ever have with him. Then I take a deep breath and let the tension out. "No, really, Color Guard's fun. For one thing, feels like I'm carrying on a family tradition, you know? Aunt Jody, you, Mumma. We got this football *thang* going on." He grins a little at that and I feel a hair better. "Of course, Mumma didn't get any of the glory, just playing flute, but--"

"Oh, she did all right. She was the smart one. Went to college, got her degree." He looks sideways at me. "She tells me you're doing real good in school. I'm glad to hear that."

The breeze coming in the window is blowing my hair all over and I scrunch it back with one hand, propping my elbow on the sill. "And I just really like doing flags. You know, all of us working together, getting it right. Of course, I'm not much good yet."

"You will be." He sits up straighter. "Just practice. Keep practicing. That's what counts, more than talent, more than skill, is how much heart you give to it. Give it everything. And put the good of the team first."

I know what he's talking about. Everyone in town knows how he wrecked his knee, playing the last minutes of the championship game. The other team's center was a big guy and he'd been beating on Dad all night. I'd heard it a million times - from Aunt Jody, Coach Gilleland; half the kids I go to school with have folks who were at the game. Last play of the night, Dad took the snap and held the ball, just held it while he waited for the receiver to get in place, held it even though that bear of a center was honing in on him. His knee snapped in the tackle, but the pass was good and they won the game. But Dad never played football again.

"Sometimes," Dad says, "you have to sacrifice. Do you understand, J.L.? Sometimes you just have to put the good of the team first and take the crappy end of the deal. Even if it hurts."

He pulls up in front of the house and shuts off the engine. I sit there, listening to the pings and sighs of the old truck at rest and Dad turns to me, laying his arm across the back of the seat. He squints a bit, half-closing one eye, thinking. Then he says, real slow, "Your mom, she's smart. She's got her act together, always did. Deserves the best. But me, I mess up and screw up and do stupid things. I hurt her real bad." He waits, gauging my reaction. "That makes me the bad guy, see? So I took my troubles out of her life, trying to make things better, staying out of her hair. But I don't come see you often enough and that makes me a bad guy again. So which am I, good or bad, do you know? Because I swear, I sure don't."

I look at him real straight and he smiles. "Lord, you look like your mama," he says, shaking his head. "Okay. I'll come to the game if I can."

"Everyone would be glad. They all say--"

"This town ain't everyone and it don't matter what they say. But I'll try." He chucks my chin and sits back, spreading both arms across the back of the seat and shaking his head. "You know that last game I played? It

170

was a night game, and raining. I remember watching the rain against the field lights, all silvery and cold. Made the ball hard to grip. When I threw that pass, the ball spiraled into the light and hung there in the air like it had all the time in the world." His gaze is far off, seeing something I can't. "It was a beautiful sight, J.L.. Just a beautiful sight."

The pre-game show is okay. We don't do anything much except make an arch for the players to run through and then do the *Star Spangled Banner* and the fight song. All the girls have their french braids and Aunt Jody has covered my head with so much hair spray I can't turn my neck without crackling. I don't see Dad anywhere.

Mumma and Brian are in the bleachers. They're probably shaking their heads over me and thinking I'll be disappointed when Dad doesn't show up. And maybe I'm a fool but there's this little burning place in my heart that keeps saying *wait, give him more time.*

But he doesn't show and he doesn't show and he doesn't show. We line up for half-time and I can see Aunt Jody and Mumma and Brian all the way across the field, sitting in the stands near the forty-yard line, just like they promised. Brian's holding the videocamera and Mumma's waving a pennant. It's so cheesy but I can't help smiling. Aunt Jody's yelling something and I can just imagine what. "Smile, girl! Show me some flash."

We march out onto the field, flags waving, fringed sashes jouncing, our heads up. Go into our routine, up, left, swirl, down, march march march. The band is playing *Rocky Top* and I finally have to face the fact that Dad's not there. I do the may-spin, overhand, two, three, four. Pivot and march, knees up high. He's not there, he didn't come, I couldn't hold onto him either. Tucker Abernathy goes into his cornet solo and I have a moment to catch my breath and then it's swing left, swing right, arc left and point. A breeze has picked up and my flag ripples and snaps. I have to concentrate, no chance to scan the crowd one more time. There's a roaring sound in my ears and for a moment, as I do the caber toss and my flag goes high in the air, end over end, I see it through a thousand spangles of light. Sometimes, Mumma said, you have to let a person be who they are. Even if they're not what you want – or need – them to be.

The flag flares and shimmers, silhouetted against the field lights and the pole drops, smack, into my hands like it's a part of me. Tears run down my face but they don't matter. I am still holding my head high.

Nature's Way

THERE WERE SOME GOOD TIMES. NOT everything my dad did was horrible. He used to take me hunting every year during deer season. We'd get ready for days ahead, washing our clothes with special soap so they wouldn't smell 'wrong' to the deer, fixing up the tree stand, cleaning our guns, buying ammo. We'd go out for a big breakfast at Mooney's, and Dad would be in such a great mood. Relaxed and happy. Carefree in a way I never saw him otherwise. "It's the best thing in the world, son," he used to say, and slap me on the back. It was the only time he touched me that didn't hurt.

Ma used to save coupons. She'd borrow the neighbors' Sunday newspaper when they were done with it and cut out any coupons she could use. Then she'd sort them into envelopes and save them up for triple-coupon days. She did this at the kitchen table after she left the Waffle House around ten or eleven o'clock at night, still wearing her uniform and smelling like french fries. Mostly she'd scoot me off to bed, but sometimes she let me help sort. Canned goods. Paper goods. Produce.

Of course, that was back when I was just a kid. By the time I was in high school, clipping coupons had become just one more thing that shamed me.

Jayelle was my girlfriend, junior year. There was something that just seemed right about her, easy to talk to, smart but not brainy. No strain on the eyes, either, and lots of fun. She could make me laugh, and I liked her folks too. They invited me for supper and served home-cooked food like spaghetti or meat loaf. They *talked* with me, you know? Real conversation. Acted like I was somebody and I began to believe it too.

Dad lost his job at the garage in October and by November, I knew my folks were in trouble. Ma began working extra shifts. Dad mooched around town, looking for any kind of work that would bring in a few bucks. He began drinking more and more and I found reasons to stay away from home. Ball practice. Going to the library to use their computers. I even thought about joining those losers in the 4H Club just to fill out Tuesday nights. Got in a couple of fights. Hung out at Jayelle's house a lot, watching TV and staying as late as her folks would allow.

But I couldn't hold things off forever.

One day I got home and Dad was in the kitchen with my sister. He was bugging her, sitting at the table

174

while she put together some Hamburger Helper. "What makes you think you could even pass a college course?" he asked, grinning with that one-eyed squint he got when he'd had a few. "Probably flunk out first semester."

My sister, who'd dropped out of twelfth grade last year, had taken her GED. "Blow it out your ass," she said, not even dropping the rhythm of the carrots she was chopping. Dad's arm shot out, as if he was going to smack her, and she pulled the knife on him. "Try it," she said. "I'm not Mom and I don't take your shit."

Dad jumped back, saw me, and grinned again. Hunching his shoulders under that beat-up jacket he always wore, he said, "Jeez, must be her time of the month, huh? Can't even take a joke." When I didn't laugh with him, he smacked me instead. I didn't even see it coming. "Wake up, boy. Can't go around half-asleep all the time."

I wanted to go at him. My fists were doubled, I was ready, but Ma came into the kitchen. "Now, stop," she said, in that same tired voice she used when trying to calm Dad down. "I'll have dinner on the table in a minute. Ben, go do your homework."

Jayelle kept nagging me about coming to my house some time. She liked Ma. "I don't expect anything fancy," she kept saying. "I could help cook dinner. I know your mom works all day. I'd just like to see where you live. Doesn't matter if it's a little messy." I knew it was a bad idea all along. What was I supposed to do, though, when Jayelle showed up after school that day with a bunch of flowers for Ma? I couldn't help thinking, *bad idea*, but I also couldn't help thinking, *Ma would love those flowers*. She would pure love them. So like a stupid ass, I told Jayelle okay, and we headed over to the house. Thanksgiving had just passed us by and Ma had draped some Christmas lights across the front porch. To me, they just made the dump look even worse and I was thankful that you couldn't really see our place from the road, just a long dirt driveway curving away behind the trees. As we came up the drive, I saw Ma running down the porch steps, carrying a big cardboard box out to her car. Clothes and shit trailed out of it and she was crying. She threw the stuff into her trunk along with a bunch of other crap in there – clothes, towels, the Mr. Coffee with its electric cord snaking out after she slammed the trunk shut. "I warned him," she said when she saw me. "I warned him if it happened again . . .". Her eye was swelling up and her nose was bleeding, and his finger marks showed red on her neck. Then Jayelle got out of the car and Ma just stopped, her mouth going slack, one hand going up to cover her eye. "I . . .I have to go," she said, and ran around to the other side of the car. She got in and began backing down the driveway. Jayelle just stood there holding those stupid flowers.

176

Dad came tearing out of the house, carrying his rifle. "No!" I screamed and ran toward him, waving my arms, like that was going to do any good. Jayelle shrieked and Dad whipped the rifle up to his shoulder, pointed and aimed. The blast nearly deafened me and I felt the rip of the bullet as it sped past my head. Jayelle shut up mid-scream like she'd been killed but she wasn't the one who got shot. Glass shattered and I turned to see a spray of red against Ma's side window as she gunned that car backwards down the driveway, spitting gravel right and left.

They always say terrible things seem to happen in slow motion and it sure felt that way. My legs started shaking and I turned around to see Dad jump off the porch and start running, that rifle still in his hands. He stopped and aimed again, and I tried to turn, tried to throw myself at him but the gun went off a second time. Jayelle dropped to the ground, screaming and holding her hands over her ears and I swung at Dad with my left fist, awkward, off-balance. I could hear Ma's car shift gears and a string of cusswords from Dad's mouth as he twisted free of me and headed across the grass, trying to get another round off before she got too far.

He cut through the woods and I took off after him. There was a clear patch where some of the cedars had broken off during an ice storm, and Ma would be a perfect target. I ran as fast as I could, legs pumping, a fucking marching band cadence running through my brain, and I launched myself at Dad as he stopped to take aim once more. I knocked him down and he swung, hitting me in the head with his rifle butt. I don't remember after that.

In the hospital they said Ma was stable. She'd lost a lot of blood, and her arm was nearly severed at the elbow, but they said she was stable. Were those people crazy? Her husband almost *killed* her. Dad was in the same hospital, different floor, different wing. Not so stable. After he knocked me out, he took off again but his feet musta slipped on the mud there beneath the trees. He fell in a ditch and his rifle went off, shooting him in the gut. They removed his spleen and part of his stomach and I guess they had to patch together his intestines, but he'll live. Yeah, he'll live.

I had a concussion, they said, and some stitches and a hell of a shiner. Jayelle had called 911. Saved all our lives. They brought her to the emergency room too, but she was fine. Just waiting to see me, my sis said. I didn't want to see Jayelle. I just wanted to go home. I wanted to go home and get ready for a hunting trip with Dad and sort fucking coupons with Ma. I wanted to know I don't have to go to school tomorrow and see all kinds of whispering and pointing fingers. I wanted my whole life to be different, as different as possible, not one damned thing the same.

Sis said to suck it up. Said I'd have to stay with Aunt Nadine for a while. Sis didn't care; she was on the phone with her boyfriend and making plans to move in with him, in his cruddy trailer. She seemed to think he'd be different, but I wasn't too sure about that. Just because he liked NASCAR instead of hunting, didn't mean a thing.

Ma was unconscious when I saw her. They had her pretty doped up, I guess. Her arm was all wrapped up. While I was looking at her, the nurse whispered "She'll be just fine after some physical therapy. Don't you worry." Easy for her to say, but who was help us through this? Pay our bills, deal with this mess? That nurse hadn't seen the look in Ma's eyes when Jayelle held out the flowers.

Dad was wide awake. They almost didn't let me in his room. Frisked me first, if you can believe that. Insisted on an orderly going in with me, some big dumb moonface asshole with pasty soft arms like a fat ragdoll. Dad was restless, his head rolling back and forth on the pillow, crying like a little girl. Tears running down his face into his beard. "Why'd she do it?" he moaned. "How could she leave me? She's all I got." He made me sick and maybe it was a good thing they didn't let me bring my pocketknife in or I mighta shoved it right then in his stupid mouth to shut him up.

There was something in his eyes, pain and confusion. He made me think of that deer, that fucking deer. The one I shot last year. My aim was bad. I got him in the knee, the right front knee, and the deer stumbled and fell, then got back up and looked at me with that same pained look, like he couldn't understand what had happened, or why it had happened to him. I never saw such a thing. The deer ran, and I stood there like an idiot, my rifle forgotten, and my stomach sick at the sight of that leg, hanging on by a strip of skin, swinging useless in an arc as the deer staggered three-legged across the road and out of sight in the woods. I couldn't imagine the pain he was in. I started to go after him but Dad touched me on the shoulder. "It's too late," he said. "You had your chance, but now it's too late. Let him go."

"But I can't, not like that! What'll happen to him?" I tried to pull away but Dad grabbed my jacket.

"Let him go," he said again, his voice quiet and still. Off in the woods, I could hear dogs barking. Barking with that kind of excited growl in their voices that makes you want to puke. "It's nature's way," Dad said. "There's nothing you can do now. Things are the way they are."

I was so pissed at him. Pissed at him then, pissed at him now. I hated the whole world.

Later, I walked down to the waiting room. Had to face Jayelle sooner or later. Had to see the look in her eyes. We went out to the parking lot. The sky was getting dark and I smelled wood smoke coming from somewhere. Under the lights, Jayelle's blue eyes were full of tears. "I'm so sorry," she said, hugging me. "I'm

180

so sorry. I had no idea. How could you deal with that for so long and never tell me?" She kissed my cheek, standing on tiptoe to do it, and wound her arm around mine. "It's so awful. Your poor mother."

"Be quiet," I said. "I don't want to talk about it."

"What are they going to do?" she asked, her face pushed up close to mine, washed with pity. "Will your dad go to jail? They won't just let him go free, will they?"

"I don't know. Just please, be quiet." I needed to get out of there. Go have a cigarette, maybe a beer. Somewhere far away, where nobody knew me.

"But what are you going to do? Do you need a place to stay? My folks said you could stay with us, on the couch, for a few days. They want to help. Our whole church does. I feel so bad for you . . ."

"Shut up, will ya?" I tried to pull my arm free. Swear to God I tried, but she held on and finally I had to do it. "Shut the hell up!" I yelled as I smacked her across the face. "Just fucking shut the hell up!"

But Who's Counting?

7:18 am

My 9-year-old and 7-year-old have 6 minutes to catch Bus 236 and ride 4 miles to PS 132. I pack 2 lunches, locate 70 cents for milk money, sign 3 papers and load up their backpacks, which seem to weigh 50 pounds each. My husband downs his second cup of coffee, aims a kiss at me, missing my cheek by 1/4 of an inch, and drives the 8 miles to work in rush hour traffic, which takes half an hour. The four-year-old turns on Channel 12 and Ernie introduces us to the number 5. I bribe my 2-year-old with 6 oyster crackers so that she will sit on the potty and do number two. I am on day 21 of my birth control pills. You know what that means.

9:27 am

I have to be at the dentist's by 10:00 so he can x-ray my number 32 molar. It will take 14 minutes, cost me $92 and I'll have to give the babysitter my last five-dollar bill. There's construction on Highway 127 and my car has only 1.5 gallons of gas in it. Three Dog Night are on the oldies station, singing "One". I'm 34 years old and all I have in my purse is $9.98 in cash, 3 sticks of gum, 4 credit cards, 1 pair of toddler training underpants, and no tissues. I graduated from college with a 3.85 GPA. Sometimes I wonder why.

11:36 am

I take the two youngest and go to K-Mart, which is having a sale. I spend $52.68 on 2 pairs of sneakers, 3 pairs of toddler jeans and a honking big box of disposable diapers. The 4-year-old tries 3 times to fit into the shelf under the shopping cart, the two-year-old manages 5 times to pull stuff off passing displays into the cart, I say "stop it!" approximately 837 times, and waste 17 minutes trying to fit into a pair of size 10 jeans. I have four kids, one husband, two cars, a dog, three parakeets and a 12-year-old house. Who cares about new jeans, anyway?

2:51 pm

My 41-pound four-year-old falls asleep in the car and has to be carried up 17 steps to her bedroom. My 32-pound two-year-old throws her 12th fit of the day and has to be punished with 5 minutes in the corner. Their naps overlap by exactly 11 minutes. I fold two loads of towels, wash 3 pairs of pantyhose, and do 20 sit-ups. My mother calls and spends 20 minutes telling me about how she won $40 by choosing six numbers in the lottery. I open a 7-Up.

4:06 pm
My older children are home from school and within 12 seconds, they dump two bookbags, two lunchboxes, 4 shoes, two jackets and about 27 papers in the living room. I count to ten. I listen to first grade reading and help practice fourth grade spelling. My son sings a commercial jingle 17 times and my daughter reveals that she has 3 boyfriends, one of whom she kissed on the elbow. I start fixing supper. Oprah is having a show about strengthening your marriage. I could tell her a thing or two about that. I've been married for 12 years. I get one "date night" a month, one video rental a week, and sex every other night. Hey, it's cheaper than counseling and burns calories, too. My husband gets cable TV and all the action movies he wants. None of them good.

5:58 pm
We get through dinner with only 2 spills, 3 arguments, and 4 spaghetti stains. Thank goodness for 409. My husband spends 7 minutes watching the sports news on TV, 13 minutes reading the front page of the paper, and one and a half minutes talking to me. Then he clears the table and I forgive him. I load the dishwasher. Three meals a day, seven days a week, 52 weeks a year. I

don't even want to do the math. I make up a grocery list. One loaf bread, a dozen eggs, large size jar of peanut butter, and coffee. Lots of coffee.

6:42 pm.

"Two, Four, Six, Eight, Who do we appreciate?" 12 cheerleaders, 9 years old, shake their pompoms and practice their cheers for PeeWee Football. My son and 16 other boys, shoulder pads dwarfing their heads, run around the field. Daughter #1 is playing hopscotch in the dirt. Daughter #2 is rolling in the dirt. Daughter #3 is at home with Daddy, pooping in her pants. I'm on Chapter 3 and just reread paragraph 4 for the fifth time. Daughter #2 whines for a Three Musketeers. I give her four Lifesavers.

8:45 pm

Three sweet-smelling, freshly bathed daughters; one surly, funky-smelling son with 7 math problems to go. My husband falls asleep on the couch 8.5 minutes after I get home. I picture to myself one large baseball bat. Then I switch the TV from Channel 9 (football) to Channel 18 (Jerry Springer) and turn the sound WAY UP. I sing two lullabies, read 3 stories, find the baby's blankie and take her on one last trip to the potty. I tell the 9-year-old four jokes and let him borrow my walkman so he can listen to 30-year-old comedy routines by the Smothers Brothers in bed. Get 4 hugs and 4 damp, noisy kisses. I give one long, satisfied sigh.

9:37 pm

I pour myself 6 ounces of wine, $6.98 a bottle. I pick up two sweaters, 3 socks, 4 naked Barbie dolls, 5 pennies, and 6 crayons. My husband comes out of his stupor and rubs my back. We have 8 hours and 23 minutes before it all starts over again. I kiss him twice. We check the TV Guide. Oh, good. "Seven Brides for Seven Brothers".

The Last Noel

KATIE SPRINGS IT ON ME WHILE I'm folding laundry. "Mom, we want to have a Christmas play again this year."

"Oh god. Not another play."

"Yes. We'll do everything ourselves this time, I promise. And no bickering."

"Wouldn't you rather just have me take you to the mall and give you all my money? Or invite a million kids over for unlimited pizza and videos? Or here, take my car keys…"

"No, Mom. A play."

I suppose any other mother would think it's sweet and cute and creative of their children to want to put on a play. Any other mother would offer to make cocoa and costumes, and invite all the neighbors to watch. Any other mother would, but not me. You see, we've had plays before.

The first year was the musical review. All-singing, all dancing. We still have the video preserving the moment when Katie, disgusted with then-four-year-old Danny's continued running through the background with a red streamer, turned around and bopped him right on the head in the middle of *Jolly Old St. Nicholas*. Ho-ho-ouch.

There was the year of *A Christmas Carol* when we ran out of costume materials and the Ghost of Christmas Future had to wear a black garbage bag for a cape. Wardrobe by Hefty Bag.

And the Nativity Play. Heated arguments over which doll would play Baby Jesus resulted in a three-way tug of war and a decapitated Tiny Tears. Possibly the only performance ever when the role of Baby Jesus was played by Kermit the Frog.

I hate Christmas plays.

Besides, the dog is sick. He is fifteen, the oldest child in the family. His sense of smell is nearly gone, he's practically blind and his hearing is worse. He has forgotten all about being housebroken.

"We're going to have to do something soon," my husband says. "You know that."

"I know. It's just . . .besides, it's almost Christmas. I don't want to spoil Christmas."

I go gift-shopping, a mammoth feat involving five hours, two malls, and a fully deployed mini-van. When I get home, I find that Coffey has been sick in the laundry room. It's the only place we can put him when we go out. The floor is smeared from one end to the other with dog feces, urine and vomit. He's covered with them too. He's wheezing and shaking, completely worn out. I know what happened. His arthritis is so bad that when he goes into a crouch, he can't get back up and he panics. I just don't know what to wash first.

Eventually I get everything cleaned up and he falls into a deep sleep. I run my hand over him and feel the ribs, fragile as matchsticks, under his coat. The vet told us over a year ago that Coffey was fading away. I just want to get him through Christmas, that's all. For the kids' sakes. All dogs die eventually, I tell myself. It's inevitable, I tell myself. Geez, I tell myself, have some perspective, he's just a *dog*.

The children are what might be called rehearsing.

"No, we're not having any singing this year. You stink at singing. We're just going to do the play."

"I don't want to do the stupid play."

"You do too. Mom! Danny won't rehearse the play!"

"I'm not doing any old stupid play unless we sing. Mom! Katie's being bossy again!"

I really, really hate Christmas plays.

189

"Look, why don't you guys compromise? Have a short Christmas sing-along after the play. Or before. Where's Becky?"

My middle child is hiding out in the den. I go in and sit next to her on the couch. "Your brother and sister are arguing," I say, leaning back and closing my eyes.

"Yep." She pats my arm. "At least they're not using fake snow this year." Through the closed door, we can hear more rehearsing. ("Freakazoid!" "Moron!") Becky cuddles up to me. "Has Santa reminded you that I really need my own TV?"

Danny is shouting in the other room. "I wanta sing carols! I'm gonna sing carols or I won't be in the play!"

"MOM!!"

No wonder Saint Nick stays Up on the Rooftop. Wonder if he'd let me join him. I'd bring my own wassail.

Coffey can't manage the porch steps any more, so I carry him out to the yard. He stands perfectly still, shivering a bit, eyes clouded with cataracts. He doesn't sniff the grass. He doesn't run, with that bunny-rabbit-like hop he used to have. His stumpy little tail doesn't vibrate with excitement.

He just stands there, face into the breeze, his eyes narrowed and gazing at something far off. A stream of pee pulses into the ground, he seems completely oblivious to it. "Come here, baby," I croon, preparing to carry him back to the house and he snaps at me, growling low in his throat. I wait until something seems to catch in his head and he recognizes me again.

"Jenny," my husband says, "you know you have to do something."

"Not yet. Soon. Not yet."

The rehearsals continue. Friends are drafted, costumes prepared, gallons of cocoa are made. Katie takes time off from directing to wrap gifts, brightly colored paper spilling across her bed as she shows me the things she bought. "Look, I got this book for Danny, he's going to love it, *Ripley's Believe It or Not*. And earrings for Becky, and this sweatshirt for Dad, and - oh! You didn't see that, did you?"

"Um, no."

"I can't even tell you who that's for. And this chew toy for Coffey. Isn't it cute?"

"Kate . . . about Coffey. . ."

Later I find her on the couch, laying next to the dog and stroking his fur. "Shhh," she says when I walk by. "He's sleeping."

The children print up tickets and programs on the computer. They plan refreshments. Rehearsals run early and late, there are always a few extra kids staying for dinner. Despite promises to the contrary, the basement is constantly in a mess with furniture shoved hither and yon, props and costume pieces stashed everywhere, and the inevitable spilled cocoa. The weather outside is frightful, but inside it's so . . . noisy. Boisterous horseplay, loud recriminations, feet clattering up and down stairs, shrieks of "Mom!". I grimly work my way through the Christmas card list and wrap gifts. Videos from previous Christmas plays are reviewed, and Kate provides critical editorial comment.

"Look at that, Becky. See how you ruined everything when you laughed during your line?"

"I couldn't help it. Danny farted, remember? It was horrible, an egg-yolkio." They dissolve in helpless giggles. "Ohhh," Becky sighs. "I crack myself up."

The video runs on, Christmas play dissolving to Christmas Eve, dissolving to Christmas morning. "There's Coffey," Danny says suddenly. "Chasing his tail. He looks like a tornado." All three kids watch the video intently, watch Coffey playing tag with a bit of ribbon, then turn and look at the couch, where he is now asleep. Becky picks up a small quilt and tucks it around him.

"I almost forgot how he used to do that," Danny says. "Remember how he used to love ice cream?"

Remember when. . .? Remember the time. . .? Remember he used to . . .? "Hey," I object. "He's not dead yet." My voice wobbles and they all turn to look at me.

192

Coffey has a bad night, trembling and crying with pain. In the morning, my husband calls the vet, makes arrangements.

"Do we have to do it now?" I ask. "Christmas is so close." We have to, he tells me. Coffey's in pain, confused, too weak almost to move. I can't stand it.

"Have mercy," Matt says. "I'll take him if you want."

No, I'll do it myself. He's my dog.

Kate hears us talking. "How can you do that? It's cruel. Would you like it if somebody did that to you? Just because he's old and sick. . ." Her face crumples and I put my arms around her. "How can you do it at Christmas? You're so mean!"

"I'm sorry," I say, wanting to smooth her hair. "I wish it wasn't like this. How do you think I feel about it?"

"I don't know! I don't care! Everything is ruined anyway. Nobody wants to work on the play, they all keep fighting. I'm just gonna hate this Christmas!" She whirls from the room, bursting into tears as she goes. Later I find her asleep on her bed, wrapped in Coffey's quilt.

Coffey is nervous in the car. He has never liked going for rides. I stroke him and murmur his name. As we walk into the office, I start to sniffle and they kindly usher me into a private room. The assistant brings a pink towel to lay on the table and I make him lie down on it. The vet has me sign a permission slip and I tell her that I want him cremated after . . . after. She gives him the shot and I hold him and talk softly to him. His body goes limp almost immediately and she listens to his heart for a minute before leaving me alone with him. I see his tail quivering and, for a minute, I think Coffey's still alive. Then I realize it is merely meaningless involuntary movements of nerve and muscle. He's not breathing. The tip of his little pink tongue protudes a bit from his mouth. I close his eyes and rest my head on his side, breathing in his doggie smell and rubbing my face against his soft, curly fur. I wish I had some tissues. After a while, I remove his collar and wrap him in the towel and walk out of the room.

It costs $50. As I write the check, the front door opens and a woman brings in a black puppy. He needs his first set of shots, she chatters happily to the receptionist, he's a Christmas present for her little girl.

When the ashes are delivered, in a very small box, the children help me scatter them in the garden. We all say a little prayer for Coffey and the kids go in the house. Twenty minutes later, when I go inside, they're in a screaming fight over revisions in the script. "I hate you!" they shriek at each other, and their doors go slam, slam, slam.

194

I keep expecting to hear him scratching at the door. Or lapping up water from his bowl. The house is too quiet. Rehearsals have been suspended since none of the cast members are speaking to each other. The Christmas tree is decorated in near silence, while the TV drones on and on. *Charlie Brown Christmas, Rudolph, Christmas Story,* the *Grinch.* Finally I can stand it no longer and order everyone into the van.

"Where are we going?"

"Crazy. And you're coming along for the ride."

I have loaded the CD player with music. The soundtrack to *Home Alone*. Bing Crosby. Amy Grant. Even, God help me, *An N'Sync Christmas*. Matt drives, circling through the neighborhoods off Highway 150, passing the houses decorated with colored lights, white lights, reindeer and Santas. Brenda Lee sings *Rocking Around the Christmas Tree.*

"Sing," I say.

"Huh? What's going on?"

"Nothing. I just want you to sing."

"But Mom, I don't want to-"

"Shut up and SING!"

Danny joins me in White Christmas. His voice is still soprano, girlishly sweet. Becky chimes in when we get to "Jingle Bells". Even Matt sings and this is no common event.

Kate is silent. She sits by herself in the back of the van, her blonde hair highlighted by the headlights of the cars behind us. Please, I pray. Please, God. Everyone else is in the middle of *The Little Saint Nick* (with four-part harmony) and my voice breaks. I have to stop singing and look out the window. Every damn house in the world has those icicle lights. The CD ends and I pop it out of the player. Rain is starting to fall and Matt turns on the windshield wipers. We listen to their slap, slap, and Danny says, "Let's sing *Conrad Suscadorem*."

"Huh? What?"

"You know. *Conrad Suscadorem*."

This has everyone puzzling until Kate, with a sigh, says, "You mean *Come Let Us Adore Him*, you dork." I find the right CD and put it in. Danny starts singing, then Becky, Matt and I. Finally, as we get to the chorus, Katie joins in. "Oh Come Let Us Adore Him, Chri-ist the Lord…" I smile at her and she gives a watery grin before turning away.

"Okay," I say. "I'm brave enough for anything now. Put in the N'Sync Christmas CD."

"You know, Mom, you're so bizarre." Becky says. "Where are we going?"

"Home. I think it's time you guys get back to rehearsing."

Another opening, another show. Becky collects tickets and shows people to their seats. Kate fusses and frets behind the curtain, double-checking her list of props. I hover nearby, getting in the way and making motherly noises.

"Relax, Kate. Everything is going to be fine. Where's Danny?"

"I sent him upstairs to get something. I decided-"

The rest of the actors are scuffling in the dressing room. I rescue my video camera tripod from the grasp of the neighbor's toddler and make a quick speech, welcoming everyone to our theater. The curtain rises, crookedly but on time, and the show begins. It is their version of *Miracle on 34th Street*, acted in full with a cast of six and frenzied costume changes.

During last year's play, Coffey kept running up to Scrooge, sniffing at his coattails and amusing the audience. My view through the videocam blurs and I frown and shake my head, concentrating harder on filming the play. Danny's hat keeps falling off, but he's an inspired Kris Kringle and Becky steals the show as the drunk lady on the phone. The audience laughs in all the right places and as the cast bows, I see Kate actually smiling.

There is a momentary confusion, then Danny steps forward, dressed like a caroler in overcoat, muffler, and knitted cap. "We would like to end this show with a sing-along. Would you all please join us?" Kate turns on the stereo and Danny leads us in song. "*The First Noel the angels did say. . .*"

The children printed programs for the play, with an addition at the last moment. At the bottom is a brief line. "We dedicate this play to Coffey. He was a good old dog. And we wish you all a very Merry Christmas."

Going to Vermont

WHEN IT IS ALL TOO MUCH, YOU can go to Vermont.

Bennington, Vermont, where the mountains are high and the air is so clean and all the carrots homegrown.

You can get off the train, suitcase in hand, long flared coat just brushing the ground. You can walk along Main Street, past quaint little shops. There is never any traffic or crime.

There's a bookstore on Main Street in Bennington, Vermont, where "signed first editions" mean Angelou, not King. You can live up above, in a one-room flat where there is space, and peace, for just you. A comfortable chair, a good reading light, shelves full of music and books. There is no phone, no need for a phone, just an unusually perceptive cat.

In the mornings you can walk in fresh snow, unbroken expanses as far as you see. When your hands start to get numb, you can stop in at the coffee shop, where the mocha grandes are always hot, where everyone knows you and nobody bothers you. You can sit quietly at a small round table to think. To read. Perchance to dream.

You keep no schedule in Bennington, Vermont. Your desk calender is clean and white, each day an unopened gift. There are no business trips to places like Topeka or Flint. No PTO meetings, no seven hundred cupcakes to bake. There are no doctor's names in red ink, next to phone numbers and inadequate directions and reminders to buy adult diapers for your mother. In Vermont, your time belongs to *you*.

Down the road, there's a restaurant where you can go to have homemade soup. They serve wine and cheese and real french bread. Sometimes they let you cook. You can slice zucchini and red peppers and no one ever says they want fish sticks instead. There is music on the radio - not news, not talk. Music that makes you sway back and forth, humming along, and if you want to sing with Aretha or Janis, no one complains. In fact, they might even applaud.

Next to the restaurant is a movie theatre, where people line up on Friday nights to watch chick flicks and foreign films and old Technicolor musicals. Nobody shoots anybody up. Neighbors greet neighbors and the only gossip is about whether the high school football team has a chance in the quarter finals. You don't have to listen to a single fart joke, or step between bickering kids. When you return to your cozy room, there are no piles of laundry on the floor or dishes in the sink. The only messes you clean up are the ones you made yourself.

It's an old town, this town, and it's slow to change. There are still covered bridges in use every day, still bright lines of maples along the roads. Newspapers are sold in the general store, with banner headlines and true-to-life pictures of the largest pumpkin grown or the annual crafts show.

It can get pretty quiet, though, in Bennington, Vermont. The four-poster bed with its piled up pillows and handmade quilt is wide and still. You can sleep all you want between the eleven o'clock news and Good Morning America. You can even sleep right through the news and if you decide to get up at two a.m. to write a poem, no one is bothered. But there's no one to welcome you back to bed, no one to wrap warm arms around you or press his face against your neck.

And so you fix yourself a cup of coffee, cradle the mug in your hands, watch the steam rise and breathe in the faint hint of cinnamon. You can sit in the rocking chair with the comforting creak and watch out the window as dawn emerges like a spring tulip, streaked with coral and gold. For this brief time, you have no moral dilemmas, no deadlines or disappointments. Just a pair of fuzzy slippers and an old chenille bathrobe that fits you just right.

You can't visit forever in Bennington, Vermont. You can go for a day, or an hour. You can stay till the coffee is cold. You can stay till you tire of talking to yourself, till you need someone to hold. Then you return to the life that you chose, where it's noisy and hectic and rich. Where little wheels fall off things and socks get lost and people think you have answers to things, as if those kinds of answers exist. You're needed in your life, not in Vermont, and if you go for too long, you'll be missed. But when it's all too much, you can come back again, and Vermont will welcome you in.

Oh! the Overnight

IT WAS SUPPOSED TO BE an adventure.

Something exciting, different. Maybe, I thought, even a bit romantic. Halfway between the Orient Express and the Twentieth Century Limited with a touch of the Flying Scotsman. You know, gleaming mahogany and shining crystal and all that.

Instead, there we were, six people in that tiny compartment on the train from Paris to Rome. Expected to spend the night together in a space even small than that hotel room on the Rue Letellier. "Strangers on a Train," I whispered to my husband. "Remember? Hitchcock?"

"I hope not," Bob whispered back. "Didn't somebody end up dead?" He returned to his self-appointed task of rearranging the luggage. Josh helped him; Josh of the Noxious Newlyweds, as I came to think of them. Heather and Josh had just been married, we found out, and were in Europe for a month long skirmish. I mean, honeymoon.

"Don't put the red case up there, it's too small. We'll lose it," Heather snarled.

"I'm not going to lose it. I'll keep it next to mine," Josh replied in perfect counterpoint. With a roll of his eyes, he explained her concern. "Our suitcases got lost coming from New York. They had a lovely tour of Germany while we were in London. We didn't get them back till Paris."

"Maybe they'll share the photos with you," I said, but no one laughed.

The bunks were divvied up, with Josh and Heather taking tops, Bob and I in the middle, and we saved the bottom bunks for *them*, that French couple. We thought it might be easier, what with him being handicapped. She would be right across from him, if he needed anything in the night. Well, of course, I thought she was his granddaughter. After all, she couldn't have been more than eighteen and he was white-haired. Anyone would have made the same mistake. I even thought it was sweet, how she took care of him - brought him into the cabin in that wheelchair, helped him into his seat, made him all cozy.

Actually, it was okay at first. We sat and talked, watched the French countryside slide away under the darkening sky, ate our sandwiches and drank wine. The French guy told us about his family's farm near Lievin, and Bob talked about fishing off the Outer Banks. Heather and Josh discussed, with increasing volume, whether or not he remembered to mail the postcards or if they were still sitting on the counter of the Hotel St. Jacques. The French girl looked out the window and I just smiled a lot.

Down the way, a group of Aussies had broken into song. "Broken" was the operative word, but they were a cheerful bunch and I longed to join them when Heather and Josh became a bit more shrill.

"You're sitting on my coat." (Heather)

"Well, get it out of the way, then. Look out!" (Josh)

"Oh great, just great! Now there's wine stains. You idiot." (Heather)

"Oh, I'm an idiot, am I? I supposed everything is all my fault." (Josh)

"I have some stain remover." (Me)

"I'm not the one who forgot the tickets and had to go back for them." (Heather)

"Fine. Just fine. I forget one thing and I'm branded for life. Josh the Fool." (Josh)

"You said it, not me." (Heather)

"Oh yeah? Why don't you just shut up?" (Josh)

"Here. Here's the stain remover. Why don't we just try…" (Me)

"Don't tell me to shut up! *You* shut up!" (Heather)

"I'm not going to shut up. *You* shut up. Just try it. I bet you explode inside of one minute." (Josh)

"Oh look! The Alps!" (Me)

Bob was no help at all. He was watching that French girl feed the old man. She was perched on the edge of the seat, carefully spooning soup into his mouth like he was a baby. The train swayed a bit, and a drop of soup fell off the spoon onto the man's lap. He gave the girl this look, this seething look, and she dropped right down onto her knees, there on that dirty floor, and put her forehead against his leg like she was begging forgiveness. My mouth hung open like a fool and so did Bob's. Our eyes met and I was sure we were both thinking the same thing. The old guy must be hell on wheels. The girl stayed there, huddled right down on the floor between the man's knees, until he put his hand on her hair. Then she got back into her seat and finished feeding him the soup.

"This is our twenty-fifth anniversary," I said, apropos of nothing. A lot of people are impressed by that. Not many twenty-five year marriages nowadays, but I got little response. "That's why we're on this trip," I added. "To celebrate."

"I do not believe in marriage," the French guy said. "It is unthinkable that people should mate for life."

"Well, you have to be able to communicate," I said. "That's the key."

"Who would want to?" he demanded. "I do not want to know all the time what someone else is thinking." He glanced at Josh and Heather. "It is immaterial to me. I prefer my little slave." And here he put his hand on the girl's leg. She kept her gaze fixed on the floor. "I say do, and she does. I say stop, and she stops. That is the way to do things." He looked at us, his eyes glittering black, no expression whatsoever, and I thought, this man has no soul.

"But…she's only a child," Bob said. "You can't honestly mean that she…"

"Oh man," Josh said, leaning forward. "You mean she has to do whatever you say?" Heather punched him on the arm.

The French man shrugged, in that expressive Gallic way. "It is her choice. She can leave or she can stay."

The girl continued to keep her face averted. My perception of their relationship was rapidly changing. "It's not a very equal partnership," I murmured.

The old man caught my eye. "There is no equality," he said. "That's foolish. She needs to be dominated."

A flush rose up my neck, into my face, as though I'd sunk deep into hot bathwater. I tried to act naturally, what else could I have done? I couldn't imagine such a life. Sure, Bob can get a bit carried away sometimes, a bit bossy, but I supposed I did the same myself. We were partners, pulling together through life. That was the way it was supposed to be, right?

The girl curled up on the bench, resting her head on the man's leg. She was just a mite of a thing, tiny as could be, built like a ballet dancer, a marionette, a stick insect. All wiry and intense, with a mop of dark hair. Not attractive, not by my standards, but something – vulnerable, I guess. Bob thought so. I could see him, watching her, getting protective. He's always gone for that, I thought. Being in charge, taking care of others. It was his thing, being responsible. It's a good quality to have, I knew, and I'd benefited from it a lot, but just then, I wished he didn't give a damn. He was changing, right in front of my eyes, from being only mildly interested in his fellow passengers to becoming a gentleman. A gentle man. Almost courtly, and with a concern towards her. When the French guy needed to go to the bathroom, Bob helped the girl. Got the wheelchair and helped get the man into it. It was sympathy, I knew, and the mild pleasure of being needed, but I didn't like it one bit.

They all went down the passageway together – the girl, the French guy, and Bob. I could hear Bob's voice, speaking to others, asking them to make way.

"Jeez, do you believe that?" Josh asked, speaking to no one in particular. "Why, that old fart. He's got her wrapped around his little finger."

"Don't get any ideas," Heather snapped. "If you ask me, she's a fool, putting up with that kind of stuff. Must be in it for the money." She opened her compact and inspected her teeth. "Wouldn't catch me taking that shit."

I looked out the window. There was nothing to see, just blackness and the reflection of the unattractive compartment. Beige walls, beige upholstery, dirty beige straps holding the upper bunks out of our way. Josh's face, alight with curiosity, could be seen peering down the passageway. Heather, sullen and annoyed, snapped her compact shut and shoved it in her purse. Rome was still nine hours away. I could hear the Aussies, bellowing some song about beer.

When Bob returned, he was smiling. "What's so funny?" I asked, and his ears grew pink.

"Nothing," he said. "Jacqueline was dancing with one of those guys from Perth." Zhak-*leen*, he said, with a French accent. I couldn't get him to say Pa-ree for Paris, but now, suddenly, it was Zhak-*leen*.

She and the man came back into the cabin, and we all got treated to the process of his removal from the wheelchair to the bench again. Bob hovered solicitously, and even fetched some bottled water. "There," he said. "All set?" I looked away, but not before that damned Frenchman's eyes caught mine, and he gave one sharp laugh, like a bark. Heather announced loudly that she needed a smoke and pulled Josh by the sleeve until he followed her to the far end of the car. I took a paperback out of my bag and tried to concentrate.

Bob's just being nice, I told myself. He's a nice man. But I couldn't forget that little look in his eye. Not

209

leering and inquisitive, like Josh, not that. And not speculative either. But it was something, a bit of warmth, that I hadn't seen in a long time. Oh, I knew well enough. No couple can be married for twenty-five years without a bit of routine settling in. And we loved each other. We did. Romance, though, is hard to retain. It seeps away, like water through pebbles. Too many things interfere. Real life interferes, with bills and children and phone calls and schedules, until all the passion has evaporated like rain in the sun. It rises in the air and is gone, and I didn't have the magic touch to pull it from the sky in a summer shower. I could be warm. I could be giving and I could be *there*, but romantic? Not.

"He's not, either." The words came out of my mouth unbidden. Bob looked at me, and I shifted in my seat. "Sorry," I said. "Reading out loud." I put the book away and cast about for some topic of conversation. "Bob planned our itinerary," I said. I received the silence I deserved but stumbled on nevertheless. "We've been wanting to make this trip ever since we got married. I have to admit, I'm envious that Heather and Josh got to do it while they're so young. Some of this is taking a bit of a toll on me." I smiled automatically, feeling my lips spreading in a puppet's grimace. "Bob's making sure we don't miss a thing, squeezing in the maximum number of tourist sights each day. We've done so much walking and I have so many blisters," I added, "that I'm beginning to think I'll return home crippled for life."

There was an appalled silence as I realized my senseless blunder. "I…I mean, I'm not used to walking so much." The man just raised an eyebrow at me, but Bob turned red and the girl stared. It occurred to me that I hadn't heard her say two words that whole trip. I plunged ahead. "Things are so expensive, too. I guess we better see as much as we can, because we probably won't be able to afford a trip like this again."

Now Bob was thoroughly embarrassed. The tips of his ears were flaming. "I think we can probably afford it if we want," he said, his voice tight. "We've managed so far. It's not like we're paupers."

"Of course not," I said in a hearty voice. "Who ever said that? I just mean that it's surprising how much some stuff costs. Like those drinks at the bistro." The bistro was my idea, enjoying a bit of sunshine at Hemingway's hangout, Les Deux Maggots. I wanted to be able to look back and say, hey, I really was there. I wanted to be able to remember a beautiful day and sparkling conversation, maybe a little handholding across the table. Instead, Bob had fussed with his calculator, figuring out the exchange rate. As if it mattered. We were in *Paris*. I think he enjoyed suffering, knowing he'd paid $8.98 for a glass of Coke. So I'd ordered two.

211

It was getting late enough, at last, to get ready for bed. We got into our bunks, laid out like stiffs in a morgue. Really, it was that bad. No light, no light at all once the door to the passageway was closed. I made sure I had my shoes nearby, under my pillow, in case I wanted them in the middle of the night. Maybe it'd be okay, maybe I'd fall asleep from the rhythm of the train, but no. I just lay there, listening to Bob snore. I could hear Heather giggling, up there in her top bunk. With all my heart, I hoped her luggage got sent to Spain.

We'd be in Rome by morning. We were supposed to go to the Vatican, first thing. Vatican, St. Peter's, the Coliseum. I'd hardly noticed the rocking of the train earlier, now it seemed overwhelming. Left-right, left-right, I could feel my insides sloshing around like a load of towels in the washing machine. The more I tried to sleep, the more awake I felt. When I first began hearing them, I thought someone was dreaming. Moaning in their sleep. Then I heard her voice, a whisper really, and a word - *Maitre*. Master.

Right underneath me, dear God, the two of them were having at it. Rustlings and whisperings, moans and heavy breathing. The air in the compartment was so heavy, dense and pressing. Bob's snores had stopped and I had visions of open eyes, each of us wide awake in the dark. My face burned and I thought, *how dare they*? Couldn't they have the decency to wait until they were alone? Was their desire so overwhelming that they couldn't resist? When certain scents began to warm my face, I grabbed my shoes and swung down from the bunk, out in the passageway in one move. I slid the door shut fast, but got one glimpse of her face. That little girl face, with her hair all wild and lips red and swollen. I wanted to slap it.

I went down near the lavatory. There was room to stand there and a light, sort of. The window was open a crack and I leaned against it, grateful for the cold air. I think I would have stayed there all night, but she came out.

The door slid open and there she was, standing under the light like the poor little match girl or something, no bigger than a minute. She walked right past me, like I wasn't even there, and went into the bathroom. I thought about propriety and passion, and that yearning look in Bob's eyes.   Just that flash in and out, and then it was gone, he was Bob again, a middle-aged man on his twenty-fifth anniversary trip with his middle-aged married wife.

She came out of the lavatory and walked right up to me. I thought she was going to say something, but all she did was open that window a bit wider and light up a cigarette. I said, "Honey, you shouldn't let him treat you like that. Stand up for yourself and he'll respect you in the end." The harsh sound of my voice startled me but I continued. "Don't let him fool you that it's love."

She shrugged, the way the French do, and looked at me. Big brown eyes, she had, and a little pointed chin and I realized, this was no child. Not an ounce of childhood in this girl. She kept staring at me. I began to feel like a fool. A big dumb hausfrau who didn't know a thing about life.

She flicked her cigarette butt out the window and leaned real close. "There are many kinds of love, Madame. More than you will ever know."

That's it. That's all she said to me. Then she sashayed back to the cabin. I was freezing out there in the passageway, shivering, so I decided it made no sense for me to stay. I went back to my bunk and tried to sleep, rocking side to side while the train shot like an arrow through the night. Left-right, left-right, slosh-slosh.

Next morning, we woke early and went to the dining car. The French couple got off the train before us, outside of Rome. I saw them from the window by our table, where Bob and I drank cappucinos and ate croissants. She was pushing the man in his wheelchair. He said something to her and she bent down over him, like she couldn't hear. Her hair fell over her shoulder, against his face, and he kissed it. Held it against his face and kissed it, tenderly. That was the last I saw of them.

Bob had been watching them too, and I saw his Adam's apple go up and down, noticed how smooth his skin was where he'd shaved, looked at his lips that used to curve. "Strangers on a train," he reminded me, nodding his head toward them. "And stranger than most." I reached across the table and stroked the back of his hand, where the knuckles rose up under warm, tanned skin and received his look of surprise.

"Do you know how much I love you?" I asked. The train started up again, moving slowly out of the station and heading toward Rome. Vatican, St. Peter's, the Coliseum.

Well, it was an adventure. Not like seeing the Eiffel Tower, not something I can hold onto with a photograph or souvenir but it was, I don't know, something I'll never forget. No, I'll never forget.

Please Leave Me My Mystique

WHEN I WAS VERY YOUNG, WOMEN wore hats with wisps of veils. Grace Kelly in *Rear Window,* Audrey Hepburn in *How to Steal a Million,* Ingrid Bergman in *The Bells of St. Mary's.* (Okay, so Ingrid was playing a nun in that picture, but you get my drift.) There was something so romantic about keeping that line of separation between yourself and the rest of the world. Nowadays, I suppose the equivalent would be little black sunglasses, but since they also conceal hangovers, there's just not the same air of inscrutability. Ah, where has all the sweet mystery of life flown?

Whatever happened to private lives, private rituals and private, er, privates? In an age when starlets' panties – or lack thereof – are front page news, is there any place for the Woman of Mystery? Everything is so public. People stand in check-out lines at the supermarket and talk on their cell phones, blithely discussing all the details of their gall bladder surgery or the latest office gossip. They fight for the chance to get on Jerry Springer or Dr. Phil, so they can openly share their most disturbing habits, their darkest secrets, and their bad fashion choices. The only real secret any more is your social security number, and even that's not safe.

Truly, no subject is considered too sacred nor too personal to keep it in the closet. Recently, I went out to dinner with my husband. At the next table, a group of teenagers were whispering and snickering about dumps. Not the kind where you take your trash, oh no, but the kind you just take. Up for discussion were the size, the shape, and the passing similarity to Hollywood celebrities dead or alive. For me, it was just WTMI – Way Too Much Information. To make it worse, those teenagers were my own.

What I want is some mystique. An aura; a hint, if you will, of the unknown. I would like to believe that when you look at me, you don't see the whole Me – that there are layers and layers beneath the surface. I'd like to be the mysterious woman, standing at a train station in the fog, cape swirling about her, whose arrival might portend any number of things. Or maybe an unexpected guest at a party whose mere presence hints at secrets concealed and reputations about to fall. At the very least, I would like you to suspect that there's more to me than my Chevy-van-Mom-mobile would suggest.

It's difficult to retain any mystery if you live in a small town, as I do. Really small town. Everyone knows me. They know my husband. They know the names and ages of my children. They know my dog. I can't go anywhere without being recognized and inevitably having someone come up to me and say, "Why, honey, was that you I saw coming out of the Weight Watchers meeting? Bless your heart." Please.

Any why does it even matter? Maybe it's as simple as this; if you believe there's more to me than looks suggest, I can believe it too. I can know there's more to my life than just going from home to office to grocery store and home again. Because there should be. For all you know, there *is*.

Yesterday, I went to the drive-in window at the bank where I've been taking my business for ages. My son had asked me to cash a birthday check sent by Uncle Jack. The teller, a new girl, looked at me and looked at the check. She said, "This is made out to someone named Daniel. Who is that?"

"My son," I said.

"Well, I can't release any funds that have been made out to someone besides yourself."

At first, I was irritated. I'd been a customer there since the branch opened, for crying out loud. And now they didn't trust me with a lousy twenty dollar check? I started to snap something to that effect and then paused. To this girl, I could be anyone. I could be a wicked stepmother, stealing the young prince's few pennies. I could be a cat burglar. I could be an *international thief.* Hey, now we were getting somewhere!

I looked at her and thought, you really don't know me....*all riiight*!!

"Thanks," I told her. "You just made my day." And with that, I flipped my little black sunglasses down over my face and drove off into the sunset, reveling in my feminine mystique. Greta Garbo, eat your heart out, dahling.

Then the Sharks

I AIN'T SCARED OF NOTHING, SEE?

I mean, people talk about courage and bravery and all that. . .well, it's no big deal. You just get up each day and go through life and you don't even know when it is you're being brave; in fact, usually you're not being brave at all, you're just getting through it the best you can and afterwards people say, gosh that took courage, but it didn't, you see? It was just plain dumb luck that you ended up looking that way.

At my age, there ain't so much to be afraid of anymore. Except maybe death and it's coming for you whether you're afraid or not. What do I care anyway? My wife's dead and my kids are grown up enough to care for themselves and my body's shot to hell so I know it ain't going to be long, so why worry about it?

I've lived through the Depression and World War II and hard times and being broke. Doesn't take courage to do it. 'Cause you got no choice, you just get through it.

Like the time my ship got sunk off the coast of Italy, back in '44. Shit, I was scared. We never even knew what hit us, all of a sudden there were the sirens going off and explosions and everybody running around like it was going to do any good and pulling on the life jackets and sliding down the side of the ship into the black water. Barnacles tore the hell out of our legs and we were bleeding like stuck pigs. And the smell of oil and salt water and fear and blood and smoke. Men calling, yelling, cursing. Then floating around and it got silent. And then the sharks came.

Yeah, then the sharks. Lured by the blood and the movement, they picked us off like cheese crackers on a party tray. We could see the lights of the rescue ship and we prayed. Lord God, we prayed. Some men tried to swim to the center, not to be on the outer ring of men, not to be pulled under and tossed up and chewed to hell. But the movement of their legs in the water just pulled the sharks closer. You could hear the screams. You could taste blood and vomit and sea water in your own mouth and you prayed God please get me out of here.

And then the rescue boats came and you tried to get there and still not move your legs and you pushed other men in front of you, just please God let us all get there, all of us. Joe and Mike and Red and Tony and Me, God. All of us, God. And you helped each other into the boat, and you cried from the sheer relief when you got in and looked at your legs and they were still there.

It got real quiet. Just those boats rocking in the almighty sea. We sat there, shivering with the cold, trying not to think, looking around sometimes, trying to see who was there and who wasn't. And then trying not to think some more.

Dawn came. Hope came. Then the Italians came and strafed the hell out of us. The captain got it and I thought we were all gonna buy it, after surviving the explosion and the water and the sharks. Goddammit. Sixty of us survived, out of over 300.

And afterwards we got ribbons and medals and they were slapping our backs and telling us how courageous we were. And then they sent us back to war.

But don't you see? Takes a lot more courage to get married and raise kids and start a business, than it does to go to war. When you go to war, you don't really have any hopes. Except maybe to survive. When you get married, you hope to be happy.

So, see, I just ain't scared of nothing. All the worst things I ever thought could happen to me already did, so I just don't worry any more. I let the doctor poke and prod if he wants, but it doesn't really matter. Me and God, we have an understanding. He knows by now that I'm not going to sit in some church and be prayed over but that I do try to do the best I can. And I know that He will take good care of Mary until I can get there to do it myself. I just want Him to take me before He takes the kids or the grandkids. That's all I ask.

When you get to be my age, people are all the time asking the secret of your success. Like there's going to be an answer they can hang onto. As if drinking the right kind of fruit juice or something will give them a long, prosperous life. I'm not so sure that a long life is all it's cracked up to be. Waking up each morning knowing you got nothing to do but look forward to your meals is a pretty piss-poor way of life. You can try to make it easy on yourself and everyone around you by being pleasant, even to the ones who talk to you like you're a toddler, but it's still a lousy payoff, to my way of thinking. But, there it is. You get up, you make a little joke, you get through it. Like you get through any particular terrifying moment of your life. You just get through it.

Bare Witness

I THOUGHT SHE KNEW.

Maybe I should have known I was wrong. I'm always wrong; wrong is my middle name, my modus operandi, my imprimatur, my stock in trade.

But I really thought that she knew.

We were drinking. We were all drinking - she, I, him, them. It was a drinking kind of night. Outside it was raining and inside we were pouring. Oh, a lot. A whole lotta pouring going on. A dusky room, with dusky blues played by a guy in a dusty jacket in a gutsy shade of green. The kind of night where talk spirals up like cigarette smoke and is just about as substantial. *He* was buying rounds.

Someone asked me to dance and we mooched around to *Miss Celie's Blues* for a while. It was good, rocking back and forth, my face pressed to a herringbone shoulder, someone's hand warm in the small of my back. *He* was dancing, too, with a new girl, and I watched her eyes light up, drink in the cognac of his attention. I knew that spirit, I'd been drunk on it more than once.

Once he'd been mine and we met in secret places and secret ways. He opened my mind and soul and heart, sliding deep into my core with a bourbon-scented whisper and a hand tugging back on my hair till my throat arched for his kiss. Rising temperatures shed my inhibitions; fevered, I sought his ministrations. I sickened for him, pulse throbbing in anticipation, naked desire making me succumb to his whims. And then he moved on.

Now I watched as he seduced the next one, and the next. A sexual beast of prey, he moved among his victims, a lion of pride. I knew him now, I recognized the moves. His games haven't gone unnoticed; whispers follow in his wake, yet there are still those who choose the adventure, invite the enthrallment. Allow themselves to be beguiled.

So, I really thought she knew. He was done with her, she was to join the rank of spectator, it was her place to look on in mute despair as he put her out of his mind. Only this time it's different, and he's the one to watch with silent astonishment as my knife slices open the empty cavity where his heart belongs and releases his flickering soul from the void.

Snap Shot

SIXTEEN HUNDRED CAMERAS. You had sixteen *hundred* cameras. For god's sake, why? Were two hundred not enough? Five hundred? At what point did you say, nope, need some more. And then, why did you stop? Eighteen hundred. Nineteen hundred and forty two. Hell, go for broke.

Over twenty thousand photos. Did you know that? Can't picture it? (Joke, hah!) I counted the damn things, dear. Went through the drawers in that oak library cabinet. Lots of little drawers with brass pulls and holders for labels. 2007. 2008. 2009. Each drawer filled with photos, divided by month, year. Photos of cars. Photos of trees. Photos of junk farm equipment sold at flea markets. Twenty thousand photos. Almost seven thousand a year. Nineteen photos a day, every day, every single day for the last three years of your life, the years after you retired. The numbers fascinate me.

Oh, and the labels. This kind of film, that kind of film. When they were taken. Which camera. But nothing about why or what. Too much to keep up with, I guess. What had these pictures meant to you? Photos of antique cars. A Packard? A Duesenburg? A 1929 Stanley Steamer with tuck-and-roll upholstery? Photos of scenery and objects. A twisted stunted tree. An apple butter stirrer, a hog snout puller. Metal carriage steps. I don't know why you took these photos. I thought it was a great hobby, something to keep you out of trouble. But it's too late now to ask and, you know, we never talked.

Your cameras go. One by one by fucking one. Sold. Auctioned. Donated to museums and universities and correctional high school vocation classes. I empty shelves, dig through drawers. Seventeen photo albums get carted away to be stored in our children's attics, on bookshelves no longer mine. I sort, sift, pick through the unlabeled photos. Send some to Uncle Orphy. Give others to antique car clubs. That lot over there might be nice if enlarged. The rest, I throw away. Shuffle them like playing cards, flip them into the wastebasket, score two points. Like I haven't got anything better to do.

Far back in the last drawer, behind the last roll of Kodachrome 400, F-stop whatever, three photos of a young woman, nude. She stares at the camera from an unmade bed, her lipstick pale, her eyeliner curving upward like Brigitte Bardot. Not professional photos but snapshots, a real person, a real room. Did you take these photos? Did you find them somewhere? What had she meant to you, a married man, a family man? I thought I knew you. *Pow.*

At last, I have the darkroom dismantled. Cupboards emptied, trash disposed. Extra film in the extra refrigerator in the extra bay of the garage has been given away. A box of stale peanut brittle, an old pair of eyeglasses, final bits and pieces of your life are swept into a small circle, scooped up with the dustpan, dumped in the bin. Photos of our kids, of you and me together, our home, your place of work, are all packed away for posterity, my illusions jammed into a very small box.

Behind a chair, an old snakeskin lies crumpled and dry, ready to disintegrate at a breath. Fine cross-hatches mark the surface, or do they simply show through the cellophane skin, an imperfect image of what went before. Do snakes wonder as their eyelids grow over with mottled golden cells? Can they tell they're about to shed baggage, excessive possessions of the biological kind? Or perhaps they give thanks with a gasp, when they finally shed that which has become too much to handle, leaving with relief the twisted, misshapen picture of what they once were.

The Last Time Dad Got Out of Jail

THE LAST TIME DAD GOT OUT OF JAIL, he didn't have any money. So Grandma told him he could stay in the old Winnebago parked in the back yard. She couldn't let him stay at the house, not with the way he smoked and her lung cancer. So I helped him pick up his stuff from his ex-girlfriend's and unpack it in the Winnie. His whole life crammed into a couple of 33-gallon Hefty bags, mostly clothes, but also fishing gear, his collection of Johnny Cash and Metallica CDs, and his football trophy. "Never borrow money from someone's purse without permission," Dad told me. "Promise now."

The last time Dad got out of jail, he didn't have wheels, so Grandpa loaned him the old pick-up truck with the cracked windshield. Dad's Jeep Cherokee still stood in Grandpa's back yard, next to the Winnebago, the hood all crushed in from where Dad wrapped it around a tree on Highway 16 South, across from the

Auto Bell. "Never drink and drive," he told me. "Promise now."

The last time Dad got out of jail, he didn't have a job, so his buddy Dwayne let him do some carpentry work under the table, which means no taxes and no child support, and I have to work at McDonald's till ten each night so I can afford my Color Guard uniform. "Never smoke pot on the job," Dad told me. "Promise now."

The last time Dad got out of jail, he got into religion. Religion and a whole new philosophy about how he was going to be a good dad, a responsible dad, a dad in charge. "From now on," he said, "you have to rely on me. You have to understand that I'm the head of this little family. That's how the Lord wants it. The man's the head of the household and the children are like little olive plants around his table. Well, you're my olive plant, honey, and this time I swear I'm going to do right by you. I'm going to take care of you now. I promise."

You know, I want to believe. I want to be able to get down on my knees and pray to God, Our Father, who art in Heaven, that I am ready to love and respect my father. But I've been promising Dad half my life that I won't fuck it up like he has and what has that gotten me? Nothing but a litany of what not to do, and damn little about what I *could* do with this messy life he's given me.

And when I come home from color guard competition, all excited because we scored second in our division, and I find Dad passed out on the couch, a six pack of beer killed and a smoldering cigarette in the ashtray, I can't help but wonder who takes care of whom, and why he's been released when I'm the one who's in jail.

Things That Happen

THE LIGHT IS STILL THERE ON THE HORIZON, he's pretty sure. Each time he crests a ridge, Mike slows the snowmobile, clears snow from his face shield, and stares ahead. It looks like it's still there, a yellow haze faintly glimmering, the town of St. Agathe. The trail has to be somewhere off to his right, but in these white-out conditions, he doubts he'll find it. Better to trust his GPS and the light. It can't be too much further. Ten or eleven miles. He swerves at the last minute to avoid a snow-covered stump and sees Jake riding on his left, wearing that stupid skunk hat and a shit-eating grin.

"You need your helmet!" Mike mouths, tapping his own to get the message across. Jake just shakes his head and Mike flips up the visor to shout. Cold air hits his face, and as he starts to yell, he realizes something. Jake isn't there. He's back at the ravine with Sammy and Domenic. Jesus! He has to shake this off. Riding through a night blizzard is bad enough without starting to hallucinate.

He has to concentrate, keep himself awake. With a wind chill factor of more than twenty below zero, he knows disorientation and hypothermia are only a hair's breadth away. The low windshield and crappy dysfunctional heated handgrips on his SkiDoo don't help. He has to stay sharp.

*

He'd taken all the usual precautions. Checked the weather, made sure his GPS maps were functional, packed repair supplies, extra food and gas, planned their route. He and Jake and Sammy were all experienced snowmobilers and although they'd never been to Montreal before, they had crossed practically every Michigan trail from Kalkaska to Marquette. It was a damn long way to Quebec, and expensive, what with gas prices and trail passes and a lousy exchange rate, but snow had been scarce this year, even in the U.P., and who knew if he or Jake would get another chance? The way things were going, he'd probably have to sell his sled after today's ride.

Even having Jake's brother-in-law along hadn't been too bad. Domenic was a full-of-shit newbie, but good for a laugh. "You gotta watch out for ravines," Sammy had told him. "They get filled with snow and you don't know they're there. I fell in one a couple of years ago, and my sled landed right on top of me."

233

Sammy pinched the bridge of his nose with a gloved hand. "Sixty percent Bondo now. My cheekbones, too. But," he added with a grin, pushing out the dental plate that held his four top teeth, "I'm thtill just as purty."

"Or just as ugly, depending on your standards," Jake said, checking the tow-hitch. He threw his gear in the back of the Explorer. With a low voice, he told Mike, "Sorry I had to bring Dom. Ever since the layoffs, Brenda's been riding my ass. It was bring him or kill her. What the hell, we'll make him buy rounds." He shrugged and pulled on his skunk hat. "How's Lisa taking it?"

Mike adjusted the tie-down straps on the sleds, checking to make sure nothing could come loose. "You know Lisa. She worries, but she doesn't say much."

"Then count your blessings, brother. Brenda just yammers, yammers, yammers. Her mouth is broken and she can't shut up." He went to check the lights on the trailer.

No, Lisa didn't say much, Mike thought. Just smiled at him with trusting eyes, believing he would find the answers, depending on him to make it turn out right. The drive to St. Agathe, an hour out of Montreal, took all day. They spent the evening in a bar watching Canadian hockey and set out early the next morning, after a big breakfast. Domenic, nursing a hangover, declined anything but coffee. The first part of the trail was easy; well-groomed, lots of curves but good visibility so they didn't have to dodge oncoming traffic too much. The rolling terrain was such a pleasure after Michigan's damned moguls and flatlands. Mike really hammered down, sending snow flying behind him so that Jake and the others had to lay back. Despite fighting wind resistance, he felt like he was flying. Free. Just him and the elements, always a win-win proposition.

"Man, that was fun," Jake said when they broke for lunch at a little hotel outside St. Jovite. "I laughed my ass off. Did you see my little buddy back there, dodging that Yamaha like a pro?" He grabbed Domenic around the neck and wrestled him down onto a bench. "Our little boy is growing up. It's so touching."

Domenic just grinned, almost shy about the praise, and pulled a flask from inside his jacket. "Any of you guys ready for a snort? I've got Dewar's."

"No drinking on the trail," Mike said. "Save it for later. We're crossing the lake this afternoon." He didn't need a drunk on the run. Domenic stowed the flask with a mutter. Well, shit, Mike thought. No one wants to be a killjoy, but somebody had to take charge. Half the snowmobile accidents every year were due to booze and half of the rest were due to water.

Before heading out again, they rechecked all their equipment and filled up with gas. The news reports called for snow in the evening but they'd be back to the hotel by then. Mike decided to let Domenic lead the pack for a while. The trail was clearly marked and they'd taken all the necessary precautions. Everything would be fine.

*

Mike reaches the top of another ridge and brings the sled to a stop. His visor is so crusted with icy snow, he can barely see. The light is still there, up ahead. Isn't it? Full darkness has fallen now. The sky is black and the snow falls in huge flakes, coming down relentlessly. His breath steams and forms crystals on his fleece face mask. He stomps his feet and claps his hands together, trying to keep his circulation going. The light *is* there, right? It doesn't look any closer. The terrain is a wide bowl with no tree line to follow and falling snow against the horizon makes him feel as if he's floating, drifting up toward the sky. Maybe the light is a mirage.

No! He has to believe it's really there. The GPS says it should be straight ahead, light from the town. The GPS is beginning to act up. The LCD screen keeps going gray. He probably should take it off his dash and put it inside his suit to stay warm, but then he won't be able to look at it while riding, and what if he got off course? Oh god, he can't bear thinking about it. They're already in trouble enough.

*

The lake was covered with ice a good three or four feet thick, enough to withstand just about anything. All along one side, ice fishing huts were set up, complete with SUVs parked outside. Snowmobile tracks led in every conceivable direction and they stayed there a while, sliding around on the ice, before hitting the trail on the other side. A half mile beyond the lake, they came to an open field area and stayed to play. Sammy performed some awesome (in his mind, at least!) spin-outs and Domenic raced Jake, handing him his ass on a platter every time. Mike couldn't stop grinning. How many times in your life did all the right elements come together simultaneously? It didn't matter what they had to go back and face tomorrow. For the moment, it was all good.

He wished Lisa could be there to enjoy it. They used to snowmobile together, before her mom got sick and needed attending. Sometimes Lisa would rent a sled, but he liked it just as well when they rode tandem, her arms wrapped around his waist. Not to mention the nights at the lodge - their bodies tired but relaxed, sex on their minds. With a little bit of cognac inside them, and Lisa silhouetted by the fire, smiling as she slowly unsnapped the front of her long johns, he'd felt complete satisfaction. Life didn't need to get any better.

After an hour or two, the surface of the field began to get mushy and it was time to head back. The fishermen were gone, their huts dark. Once on the lake, it took a while to find the right entrance back onto the trail. There were so many to choose from and they cruised along the shoreline until they spotted another group of sleds entering a trail through a gap in the trees. Hopefully, those guys were locals and knew their way around. The temperature dropped swiftly. After about an hour on the trail, Mike was beginning to wish they'd spent less time on the field. They could have been back at the hotel by now, soaking in the hot tub, throwing back one scotch after another. Sammy drove in front. His eight-year-old Polaris had been coughing and hacking a lot, probably carburetor gunk, so the going was slow. Domenic followed him, then Jake, and Mike brought up the rear. The snow dust kicked up by the sleds hung so thickly in the air that they had to allow nearly a quarter-mile gap between them in order to have any kind of visibility. The pack of sledders they'd followed onto the trail had disappeared long ago.

Sammy's Polaris completely gave up the ghost thirty minutes later. They abandoned it and he rode double with Domenic, whose rented Arctic Cat had the best headlights. Soon after, the wind became even stronger and they all had to stop again to don heavier gear – fleece face masks, extra layers under their jackets, heat packs in their gloves and boots. They got underway again, but within a couple of miles, Mike realized they'd lost the trail. They must have missed a turn or something. There was still a trail, but it wasn't the wide, groomed version from that morning. Instead, it was narrow and rocky, with overhanging brush and no signage. Shadows were getting long and they hadn't seen any other traffic since leaving the lake.

"I think we're on a private trail," Mike shouted when they stopped once again. "A lot of clubs around here probably blaze their own." He had to raise his voice over the shrieking wind. "We need to go back."

"Hell with that," Sammy shouted. "What does the GPS say?"

"I don't have the software for Canadian trails. I don't even know if any exists. I just have towns and highways, rivers and lakes."

"Oh great! That's just great! When were you going to tell us that? After we fucking froze to death?" Sammy climbed off from behind Domenic and stomped his feet, crossing his arms over his chest and tucking his hands into his armpits. "Damn, it's cold. Dom, you got any of that Dewar's left?"

Domenic pulled out the flask and handed it over. "Uh, listen guys," he said, "how much further do you think we've got? Because I'm getting low on gas." He scraped snow off his fuel indicator. "I think the extra weight has cut into my gas mileage."

No shit. The gauge stood below the quarter-tank mark. They lost more time siphoning gas out of Jake's sled and into Domenic's. In the meanwhile, Sammy put away a good bit of scotch. "It won't help if you get drunk," Jake yelled, coiling up the siphon hose and packing it away. "Wherever we are, we're on some kind of trail, and sooner or later, it'll lead back to the main trail. But it might be sooner if we backtrack."

"Yeah, but then we'll have to cross the lake in the dark. You want to do that? We could spend all night trying to find the trail on the other side." Sammy screamed his words, steam roiling from his mouth, the sound getting whipped away by the wind. He slammed his helmet mask back into place and climbed on Domenic's sled.

Domenic, who'd been pretty silent since leaving the lake, said, "Does anyone have a power bar or something? I'm feeling kinda shaky. Diabetic, you know."

Jake rolled his eyes and dug in his fanny pack. "Here's some peanut M & M's. That ought to hold you. Now let's hit the road. It's almost four o'clock, we're gonna run out of daylight."

*

This shouldn't have happened, Mike thinks. This is why you plan and prepare and don't take too many risks, so you don't get caught with your pants down. But, damn it, things *do* happen. That was what Lisa had said. "You can't control everything and you can't blame yourself. We'll be okay."

Yeah, sure they would. The auto industry was fucked, which meant new construction was fucked, which meant plumbing suppliers were fucked, which meant he, as plant manager, was fucked. Things happen all right. But this shouldn't have.

He checks his cell phone again. Still no signal. Up ahead, that faint smear of yellow light on the horizon. He thinks about Jake and Sammy and Domenic, huddled in the ravine, trying to erect a windbreak, probably talking a lot of nonsense to keep each other awake. They're counting on him to get help, to make sure they don't freeze to death, disappear forever from the face of the earth. He can't fail.

But he could. This is what Lisa doesn't understand. He *could* fail. Despite all her faith in him, he might not find the right path to get them out of trouble. He isn't God. Hell, he doesn't even believe in God any more. Was God going to help him out? Buy his house? Pay off his mortgage? "If things get too bad," Lisa said, "maybe we could go to your father." Ha! It'd be a cold day in hell before he looked for help from that sorry son-of-a-bitch.

Maybe it was already too late. Maybe they should have left Michigan years ago, gotten work down south or out west. Now, they stood to lose their home, their cars, everything. They could lose *everything*.

Mike feels the sled heading downhill, into another valley, and he rises up slightly, standing on his pedals,

241

trying to see beyond the next ridge. Suddenly, *bam*, just like that, he's on his back. The sled flies out from under him, cuts right, and goes over on its side. The tethered kill switch ensures that the engine shuts off, but the headlights stay on. He's hit something, a tree branch maybe, something high across his chest. For a moment, he just lays there, stunned, trying to catch his breath. He slowly turns his head. Barely detectable is a guy wire running to a utility pole. Snow clings to the side of the pole, rendering it nearly invisible. If he had been sitting instead of standing, if the guy wire had hit him just a few inches higher . . . Mike swallows, and swallows again.

Gradually, he takes inventory. Legs, arms, they're okay. He tries to roll over and immediately pain strikes. Cracked rib, maybe. It's difficult to take a deep breath. He holds one arm tight against his side and slides on his back over to the snowmobile. An inch at a time, he works himself up into a sitting position, resting against the overturned sled. Shit, he thinks. Shit, shit, shit, shit, shit. This is bad.

He checks his cell phone. No signal. Is he *any* closer to the town? God, he hopes so. He needs to tape his ribs and then he needs to lift the sled. Trouble is, all his tape has already been used on Jake.

*

The ravine was so snow-covered, they didn't see it. Jake skidded for a second along the edge, then plunged in sideways. It took all three of them to get the sled off him, basically hitching it to Domenic's sled and dragging it out.

Jake's hip was broken. They were pretty sure of that. Sammy was a chiropractor and he was able to put Jake's leg in traction, rigging up a makeshift pulley and weights. By that time, though, Jake was soaked with sweat from fighting the pain and a lot of time had been lost. They managed to get an insulated, waterproof ground pad beneath him but there was no way to lift him out of the ravine. "Besides," he said, his voice shaking with cold, "what difference does it make? I sure can't travel. You guys have to go get help. They'll need to helicopter me out."

Domenic and Sammy were sober-faced, the whites showing around the edges of their eyes. They dug out everyone's emergency supplies – insulated blankets, flares, flashlights and batteries. "Keep Jake warm," Mike said in a low voice to Domenic. "Wrap him up and then try to set up some kind of windbreak."

Sammy investigated Jake's sled. "Shot to shit," was his verdict. "Front left suspension's kaput." He glanced around helplessly and swore. "Guess it's up to you, Mike. Domenic and I will both stay with Jake."

"Why? What good will that do?" Dom's voice broke and he looked like he was about to crap his pants.

243

"I'm not any help here. I'm an accountant, for chrissake. Let me go with Mike. My sled still works."

"You'd ride off and leave us with nothing, asshole?"

"Then I'll double up with Mike!"

"Yeah! And use up all his gas, too! Jake's your own brother-in-law, for chrissake. Stand by him!"

"Stand by him yourself, Sammy! I'm not being left here to die!"

Sammy launched himself at Dom and the two men rolled over in the snow, grappling and cursing. Mike dove between them, getting his helmet wrenched painfully to the left in the process. "Nobody's going to die!" he shouted, kicking Sammy loose and pinning Dom to the ground. "Don't go all ape-shit on me now! We need to think this out."

They lay in the snow, groaning, breathing hard. Dom and Sammy refused to look at each other. Jesus, Mike thought, why the *fuck* do I always end up in charge? I don't need this. He crawled over to Jake's side. "How you doing?" he asked softly.

Jake's gaze was steady. "All things equal, I'd rather be in Cheboygan." His smile slipped away. "It's bad. We're in trouble."

"Trouble? I was born in trouble. Trouble's my middle name. And all this time, you thought it was Andrew." Ah hell. There was no way to make light of things now, and no time. He gripped Jake's gloved hand. "I'll bring help," he promised. "You just hang tight. I'll bring it."

He stood, squaring his shoulders and pulling on his gloves. "I'm going alone," he announced. To Sammy and Domenic's immediate outburst, he simply shook his head and started up his snowmobile. "You guys work things out, damn it. Keep warm. Hang onto the flares and shoot one off every hour. Just one! Gather some wood and build a fire. I'll be back as soon as possible."

*

Mike unhooks the GPS from his sled and holds it close to his face. Nothing. The screen is a blank gray, the deep cold leaving it useless. He has absolutely no idea which way to go. The horizon has disappeared. He'll have to feel his way to the top of a ridge before he has even a prayer of seeing the light from town. Tucking the GPS inside his Jakeet, hoping his body heat will bring it back to life, Mike struggles on in knee-deep snow. His breathing becomes more ragged. A weight pulls at his lungs, keeps him from drawing a deep breath and he stumbles repeatedly, groping his way uphill. Somewhere ahead, he hopes, is St. Agathe, with light, warmth, and emergency medical teams. Somewhere behind is his friend, Jake, the guy who's been his best pal for twenty years, and Dom and

245

Sammy - quarreling, unreliable, scared. Beside him, inside him, Lisa takes care of her mom and waits to hear, ready to welcome him home.

He keeps walking. Each step a conscious effort. Each step a reminder that he can't fail, that three other lives depend on him. He checks his cell phone again. Still no signal. Things happen, he tells himself, that you can't control. All you can do is keep trying, keep walking. Lisa knows where the important documents are kept, if necessary. House insurance. Life insurance. He wonders if she can feel him thinking about her now. He wonders if she'll know how hard he tried to get back home. If she'll know how hard he tried. "Help me," he whispers. "Someone please help me. Let there be light be on the horizon."

Litter Box Full

CATS. HE HATED HIS MOTHER'S CATS and no sooner did he unlock the door to her house than three of them appeared and began mewling and twining around his legs. Tim nearly tripped and his foot came down heavily on one of the cats' tails. Tallulah yowled and leapt across the room, jumping from chair to table to top of the bookcase, spitting and swearing at him as she ran. "Yeah, whatever," Tim said. "Watch where I'm going next time."

He dumped cleaning supplies on the kitchen table and opened all the windows, north and south, despite the chill January air. Anything to dispel the ammonia fumes. The litter box, pan and all, he dropped into a garbage bag and took outside. After the floor had been swept and mopped and dried, Tim put down a layer of newspapers and a brand new Litter Maid Mega self-cleaning litterbox, advertised on TV as 'ideal for multiple cat households'. Four cats lined up on the kitchen counter, watching him. He could feel the itch starting at the back of his throat, that little tickle that would turn into a cough and runny nose and weeping eyes. Tallulah was still out in the living room, apparently nursing her grievances. Or maybe just pooping in the window planter. Tim opened the fridge and cleaned out the leftovers, dumping them into another garbage bag. Spencer, the tabby, dropped down to the floor and touched his pant cuff with one paw.

"Hungry? Tough." Tim washed off the table, collected all his mom's pill bottles into a ziploc bag, closed the windows.

He entertained the notion of letting the cats wait another day, too, letting them just wander around hungry and thirsty, letting them suffer a bit. Shoot, they'd probably just make a worse mess, to get back at him. Tim refilled the water dish, measured out the prescribed amount of Whiskas.

"When are you guys gonna pull your weight around here, hmm? Like maybe learn to dial 911?" Lucy and Ethel were the first at the food, Spencer holding back and Clark pretending he wasn't interested at all. Tallulah strolled in as Tim left the kitchen, her tail twitching disapproval. "Don't get high and mighty with me," he said. "I'm the one who keeps you alive."

His mother's bedroom was dark, shades drawn, bed unmade. Framed photos of John Wayne and James Dean stared down from the walls. He started to pull clothes from the closet but everything he touched was covered in cat hair. The bathroom door was still closed and Tim decided it could wait a little longer. Little goose bumps rose on his arms and he left, coughing as he locked up.

At his own apartment, he dropped his clothes in the hamper, showered, stood under the spray gargling, trying to get the oily residue of cat out of his throat. He shaved, dressed, shopped. When he got to the hospital, he found his mother leaning against the doorway of the nurses' station, her hair filthy, eyes flat. Tim leaned down and kissed her cheek, his lips feeling the sharp angle of her cheekbone, the deflated texture of her skin. "How's it going?"

She looked into the K-Mart bag he'd brought. "These aren't my clothes."

"They're all fresh and new, though. Thought it might cheer you up."

"Little late for a make-over. I want my own clothes." She took the bag and disappeared into her room.

Tim stuck his hands in his pockets and went to the recreation room. Several patients watched TV or played cards. One or two looked familiar, from other times, but then those people all tended to look the same. He could almost spot-diagnose by now. Darryl the Drunk, Cleo the Clinically Depressed, Schizophrenic Sue. He wondered what today's therapist would be like. Nurse Ratchet? Or one of those happy-hugger types? Maybe an oh-so-serious straight-talkin-kinda guy, like in

'Twenty Eight Days'. Too bad there wouldn't be a Sandra Bullock among the patients. Just his luck.

His mother appeared in the doorway dressed in navy sweatshirt and jogging pants, her wet hair piled on top of her head. "They're too big," she said. "How do I look?"

"Like Kate Hepburn in 'Pat and Mike'. All you need is a little towel draped around your neck."

"I liked her better in 'Desk Set'." She sat on the couch, her gaze darting about the room. Her eyes had that funny look again, the whites showing all the way around, and she kept touching the edge of the wrist bandage under her sleeve cuff. "Everybody talks about 'Philadelphia Story' but I always thought her later stuff was better. She was more herself, more comfortable in her skin. Did you feed the cats?"

"Yes. As God is my witness, they'll never be hungry again."

Group therapy was held in the dining room with the tables pushed back. He hated that. Why did they have to sit in a circle, it was awkward. Why couldn't they have a table, like dignified people, like executives? He never knew what to do with his hands. This time the therapist was a big guy with a deep voice--Sal. He looked like a football coach. Already, two of the middle-aged ladies were perking up, touching their hair. Coach began the session with introductions, going

250

around the circle, everyone expected to give a condensed version of their particular sob story, family members encouraged to join in.

Tim did five minutes on cats in his best Jimmy Stewart. "And-and-and so I said to the cat, Mr. Jinkers - that's his name, you see, the cat's. Mr. Jinkers. I said why do you look at me like that? I'm doing the best I can. But that's the thing about cats, they don't care, they just don't . . . CARE . . .and-and-and I asked why won't you do …whatever is you're supposed to do… in the catbox and just . . .do it. Just-just-just . . . DO it." Little grins lit up around the room and he enlarged his gestures. "Did I ever introduce my friend Harvey?"

Coach Sal was not amused. "If you had one thing you wanted to say to your mother, Tim, what would it be?"

Tim turned to his mother and looked deeply into her eyes. "Why-why-why couldn't you get a dog, Mom? A little . . .DOG." The place cracked up. His mother smiled too, her gaze fixed on Coach's shoe. Tim's chest tightened. It wasn't his fault . He hadn't dumped her the way Dad had, he hadn't moved to Florida like his brother, Jack, just to stay out of reach. He was the good guy, damn it. He was the one who stayed.

"And Rosalind, what have you got to say?" Coach asked. "Nothing? No?" She shook her head, her smile tightening.

After the session was over, they walked to the exit

251

and waited while sign-out sheets were completed and the nurse had unlocked the door. "They give you any idea when you can come home?" Tim asked. "How long was it last time?"

" I don't remember." Her gaze flitted past his shoulder. " Don't forget Talullah's medicine. Stroke her throat to help it go down."

"Yeah. You be a good girl and take yours too." He kissed the top of her head. "Good-night." She walked away, veering off-center like a blind woman.

On Sunday Tim ran into his mother's apartment long enough to grab her clothes and feed the cats. Little hunks of cat shit encircled the new litter box, while the sand within was pristine. "Goddamn it," he snarled, taking a swipe at Lucy sitting on the table. She skittered sideways, up and over the chair back, down the hall. Ethel appeared, wide-eyed, in the kitchen doorway, took one look at Tim and flattened herself, squeezing behind the utility cart. Tim grabbed a roll of paper towels and cleaned up the poop, gritting his teeth at the feel of the cold lumps under the quilted picker-upper.

"You guys just don't get it, do you? I'm not going to clean up your messes forever. You think I don't have better things to do?" He got the squeeze-bottle of cleaning solution and spritzed the floor, getting down on his knees to scrub away the mess. "You think I can do this forever? I have a life of my own, you know.

Enough is enough." He slammed the broom closet door with enough force to rattle the pans in the cupboard, and all the cats disappeared.

The silence was total. After the echoes of the slammed door died down, not a sound existed in the house. No traffic from the street, no TV or radio. Not a clock ticked. The cats, wherever they were, seemed to be collectively holding their breath. "Oh dammit," Tim sighed. He refilled the water and food dishes. No cats. "Here, kitty, kitty. Come eat." He whistled a careless little tune, jingling the keys in his pants pocket. "C'mon, Tallulah. Drag your flea-bitten carcass in here, I gotta give you your medicine." Still nothing. Tim swore and grabbed the bag with his mother's clothes. "Fine. Be that way."

His mother lay in bed, her face turned to the hospital wall. A chenille bedspread, thin and missing tufts, a bilious green, was pulled up high over her shoulders. "Time for group therapy," Tim said. "Come on, Pilgrim. We're burnin' daylight."

"I can't." Rosalind's voice was muffled. "Go home, Tim. Go out with that nice girl. What was her name? Ellen? You still going out with her?"

"No. She's been busy. Eh, what the hell, she didn't know her Garson from her Grable. Come on, Mom. If I can drive all the way over here and take time from work, you can walk twenty feet to the dining room. You can't just give up. Think of Susan Hayward. Did she

253

give up in 'My Foolish Heart'? Or Julie Walters in 'Educating Rita'. Did she let a little depression get her down? What about Sandra Bullock?"

"Fuck Sandra Bullock." His mother flung back the bedspread and sat up. Her topknot had slid sideways, loose wisps hanging over her face. She still wore the navy blue sweatshirt, now with stains on the front. "I don't want to go to group. I don't want any more stinking fish sticks for lunch, and I DON'T want to be in this PLACE! Why can't you just leave me alone?!" Rosalind threw herself back down on the mattress.

A nurse came to the doorway. "Not having a good day, are we?" She leaned over Rosalind, patting her shoulder, and spoke to Tim. "She'll be better when her meds kick in. Why don't you come back later?"

Tim walked out of the room. Other patients were gathering in the dining room. "How's Harvey today?" one of them asked. Tim kept walking, bumping into the information table against the left wall of the hallway. A stack of brochures labeled "FAMILY THERAPY, Westport Medical Center" fell to the floor. He crouched down and picked them up, one by one. At the nurses' station, he realized he still held the bag of his mom's clothes and handed it over to the blonde RN with the downturned mouth.

Two cat turds in the living room. Three in the hall. A pool of urine by the back door. And in the litter box, the surface of the clumping media was still undisturbed. He grabbed the Litter Maid Mega and ripped the paw-cleaning-ramp off the front. Sprays of Fresh Step went right and left, the sealed waste receptacle clattered to the floor. Tim broke the mechanized rake over his knee.

"You goddamned freaks of nature! You spawns of hell! You won't even try, will you? Well, fine, see if I care any more!" He threw the litter box out the back door, watching it cartwheel across the yard. Energized, he grabbed a bucket, filled it with hot soapy water and unlocked the bathroom door. His breath came in huffs as his eyes began to itch and sting.

Most of the blood was in the bathtub. Black now, congealed, it covered the white ceramic and the pink rubber mat. A sluggish river of shampoo meandered through, heading for the drain. Red finger-prints stippled the edge of the tub, black scuff-marks showed on the tile floor and along the baseboards. The white rug was ruined; he threw it in a garbage bag, along with towels and his mother's robe. Strong odors rose up as he turned on the sprayer - metallic, bitter-edged -- along with the floral scent of Dove soap. Tim used a scrub brush, the old-fashioned kind with stiff bristles and wooden back. Used both hands, got on his knees.

"Damn it, damn it, damn it," he said over and over, rinsing the scrubber, coughing and sneezing as his allergies kicked in. His throat just wouldn't clear and he began to wheeze and the more he wheezed the madder he got. "Fucking mess, fucking goddamned mess," as his eyes itched and tears streamed down his face. Blood had seeped into the cracks of the tiles around the toilet.. He was sobbing now, rocking back and forth on his knees, nose running. His elbow caught the can of cleanser and knocked it flying. A cloud of pale aqua powder filled the air, coating his arms, face and shirt. "No wire hangers," he said and the tickle in his throat erupted in laughter, then he slumped against the toilet. "No more wire hangers. Oh god, I'm going crazy too."

Finally the room was clean. Every surface sparkled, bottles and jars were lined up with precision on the counter, even the toothbrushes stood at attention. Tim rinsed off his hair and face at the kitchen sink, threw his shirt away and sat down in the rocking chair in the living room. His t-shirt was wet in splotches and his trousers and shoes were filthy, but the bathroom was clean. Lucy and Ethel popped their heads up from behind the couch. "Hey, girls," Tim said. "How's tricks?"

He'd have to go home and shower before going back to the hospital. First he swept up the kitchen again, put down newspapers, found an old plastic dishpan and filled it with kitty litter. "Work with me, guys," he whispered. "I'm doing the best I can." Talullah sat on the windowsill, performing her ablutions. Tim got her under his left arm, pried her mouth open, and shoved the pill in. With his left hand, he clamped her mouth shut, with his right, he stroked her throat. "You know you need this," he said. "Just meet me halfway." She shook herself all over when he released her and walked off tail in the air. "You're welcome," Tim called after her. "Any time."

His mother was dressed when Tim got there, in her own clothes, sitting curled up on the couch in the recreation room, watching reruns of 'Columbo' on TV.

Tim dropped down next to her. "I finished cleaning your apartment.

"No one asked you to." His mom reached over and grabbed his arm before he could pull away. "Sorry. God, I'm sorry. Don't know why I get like this. I'm so tired." She leaned over and looked in his eyes. "You don't deserve this."

"Neither do you. But damn, you have to try. We all have to get up each morning and try. You're a beautiful intelligent woman with lots to give. You think it's easy for me to watch you go through this?"

"No. But it's no picnic from my side either." She sank back into the couch and closed her eyes. "How are the cats?"

"They won't use the litter box. I can't understand it. I wish they could just speak up and say why."

"Wouldn't help. They don't know why. They're cats." She took a deep breath and looked up at him.

"You just keep coming back, don't you?"

"Little Sheba, that's me." Tim let a small smile curve his lips, but he held her gaze.

Rosalind patted his knee. "Well, we always have Group to look forward to. I hear the topic tonight is Controlling Your Environment. Sounds like a laugh riot."

"You never know. Maybe it has a happy ending. Something heartwarming with Barry Fitzgerald. 'Going My Way'. 'The Quiet Man'."

"'Drums Along the Mohawk.'"

"No, that was his brother, Arthur Shields."

"Are you sure?"

"I'm sure." Tim put his arm over his mother's shoulders. "Now, 'How Green Was My Valley', that was Barry Fitzgerald. You ready?"

"The show must go on. I guess."

Tim winked at her. "Here's looking at you, kid."

Cello, Standard

JACK WATCHED AS VALERIE PACKED for her trip. Heavy, hard things in the duffle bag. Soft folded clothes in with the cello. She filled crevices with rolled socks and wispy panties, padded the fingerboard and tail piece with blouses and sweaters. "I wish you'd let me come along," he said.

"No. I'm too nervous." She was humming again, Bach Suite No. 1 Prelude. Slurred, choppy, smooth and deep, all the various ways she'd practiced it over and over the past month.

"You'll be fine," he said. "An asset to any program."

"Right. And the other students can call me Granny." Frowning, Valerie slid her audition outfit into the garment bag. Navy silk, demure as hell until she spread her legs for the cello, when hidden slits would reveal her slim calves, her graceful high-arched feet. "Besides," she added, "I want to keep Baby in the front seat next to me." She patted the cello, momentarily caressing the curves.

The cello case lay across their bed, flapped open, the red velvet lining in stark contrast to the white bedspread, the cello itself a deep glowing brown. For a year now, Jack had shared his home with this entity, living wood, and with Valerie, all warmth and color and life. "You need me," he said, fists balled up inside his pants pockets. "At least to help with the luggage. Deliver coffee. Provide massages. Your personal cheering section."

Valerie stopped what she was doing to climb on his lap. Straddled him, looping her arms around his neck. "I'll be back, you know. Before you can miss me."

"I already do. Besides, they'll accept you and then you'll stay out there." Valerie shook her head but Jack held her tight. "Yes they will. You've practiced so hard. You care so much. They can't not take you."

She kissed him. Lips, jaw, his closed eyelids. "You're sweet," she said, "but for God's sake, grow up."

They met at the music store. Valerie had been weighing the merits of a Yamaha electric travel cello. "Weighs less than ten pounds," the salesman had assured her, "even with the travel case. And you can take it anywhere." He set it up, plugged it in. Without the wood body, all that exists is the cello's stringboard and head, fold-out side pieces to balance between the cellist's thighs, and a chest rest.

"Looks like a praying mantis," Jack had joked, forgetting the pretense that he wasn't eavesdropping, hoping to bridge the gap between classical and rock, between cellist and drummer, between yin and yang.

Valerie had smiled and, seating herself, drew a bow across the strings, playing a few notes of Verdi. "Nice buzzy tone," she said. "I like it. Good upper harmonics. But not for me."

"Maybe you should get it," he'd pushed. "If you have to go back and forth to classes on the bus, it'd save you a lot of hassle. Make things easier."

"No, I don't think so. Easy isn't always better." She tossed her keys in the air and caught them again. Her ponytail stuck out the back of a baseball cap, on which was the legend *Bach is My Homeboy*. Jack closed his eyes on the image of himself, wrapping his hand around that ponytail, pivoting her face toward him for a kiss.

He opened his eyes again to see her smiling at him, as if she'd read his mind. "Some things aren't supposed to be easy," she teased, sauntering close enough that he could smell her perfume. "They've got to be real."

Jack took her to a series of dinners, then a concert, and finally to bed. Before they made love for the first time, she had drawn her hands up her body, pausing a moment to stroke herself. *Pizzicato*, she whispered, and then she licked her fingers. Sucked her own juice greedily before letting him taste her, before opening her thighs and letting him in.

Jack woke in the middle of the night. Valerie's side of the bed was cold and he could hear the shower running in the bathroom. She must not have been able to sleep – the cello case lay open on the carpet and she'd clearly been re-arranging the padding – a blouse had been replaced by a cashmere scarf, blue lace panties had been wrapped around the bow. Her lucky panties, she always said. She believed in luck. Serendipity, fortuitious chance, hunches. She had even washed the car that afternoon, just in case. "In case of what?" Jack asked, knowing, and she grinned.

"In case the director happens to see me getting out of my car before the audition. He might say, What a clean car! I want that girl in my classes!" Then her smile had disappeared and she shrugged. "Have to try. Even though the odds are bad."

"You'll make it," Jack told her again.

"Might not. Might be me and Baby, sawing away alone until we reach the absolute bottom and, you know, give lessons. That would be *major* suckage." Her tone had been light, but when she turned away, Jack saw tears.

Everything rode on this audition. At least that was what she thought, he knew. There was no other plan for her, no options, no fallback position. He felt sick, his stomach shrink-wrapped to his spine. If she got accepted into the program, she'd move to Boston. He could follow, sure. A good drummer can always get a job. But in Boston, in that richer atmosphere, she'd grow away from him. It would be a case of classic versus contemporary, Bach versus rock. She'd grow serious, even more dedicated to her craft. He could see it now, a prophecy. If she got this job, she'd leave him.

It was that cello, that damned massive wooden cock between her legs! It wasn't even a classic or antique, just a standard cello from a catalog. She hadn't been able to afford more. He remembered the first night they made love, when she had driven him crazy with her touch, stroking him until he vibrated, playing him until he reached crescendo. And then afterward, as he lay there and the sheets cooled, she went to the living room and he found her there, nude, playing Vivaldi in the moonlight. After that, he had no choice.

The wisp of blue lace caught Jack's eye and he pulled the panties free of the bow. Held them to his face while his senses filled with her scent. He could hear the water still running in the bathroom, and Valerie's voice, humming the opening notes to the D Major Sarabande. Quickly, he pulled all the clothing loose from the cello. He lifted it from the case, stood it between his hands. A

263

little pressure, just a bit, and the wood could crack. No one would know. She'd pull it out to warm up before the audition and she'd hear it, a little sigh as air passed out of the cello's lungs, and she'd lose confidence. It would be there in her eyes, like Sasha Cohen before her long performance in the Olympics. The self-fulfilling prophecy that she'd fail. Valerie would come home from the audition, desperately sad, but he'd make it up to her. He'd love her enough to make it up.

In one hand, he still held the panties. She'd been wearing them the day they met – that's why she said they were lucky. "Who'd have thunk," she told him, "that we'd find each other out of all the people in the world? It was meant to be." He held the panties and he held the cello. One moment of leaning to the side, one decision to make, one split second to change his life forever.

"Oh!"

Valerie stood in the open bathroom door, a towel wrapped around her. She stood perfectly still, taking it all in. He hadn't done anything yet, but in that moment of perfect clarity and self-fulfilling prophecies and pure bad luck, he knew that she knew what she knew. And he knew it was over.

No Anchovies

I MEAN, IT WASN'T EVEN VERY GOOD PIZZA.

Of course, pizza is pizza, and everyone has his or her own idea of what makes good pizza; for some it's the crust and others it's the sauce or the cheese or the meat. I like a good pan pizza myself but my husband says that pizza is like sex. When it's good, it's very very good but when it's bad, well, it's still not that bad. Better than getting hit in the head with a sharp rock, he says. I mean, if I'm going to have sex at all, I want it to be good sex. I mean pizza.

We ordered the pizza in the first place because we were so tired after driving home from the city. You know, all that traffic and the dust from the road crew settling on the car right after my husband washed it on the weekend and the deejay on the radio telling those moronic jokes and the commercials.

I don't usually go into the city, there's a nice shopping mall right nearby with everything that I most usually need, but this time it wasn't shopping that I had to do. No, instead we were at an office, one of those big offices in the tall buildings right in the center of town where you can never find a parking space because they're all either taken or too small or have a sign saying restricted or handicapped. When you think about it, any woman trying to park in a parking space and get out with her purse, a diaper bag, a baby and a toddler is pretty darned handicapped. That's what I think, and someday I hope to see a parking space with a sign saying pregnant ladies' parking only.

Of course, when we got to the office, we had to wait in the waiting room, wait where there were a dozen other ladies with babies, toddlers or preschoolers, and all of them, every single one, had a runny nose. Not the ladies; the babies, toddlers and preschoolers. I had to keep telling my toddler not to touch things and, of course, he touched things. I had to keep washing off his hands with those little wipey things and that meant I had to keep digging in the diaper bag, which is not easy when there's a baby on your lap and another pretty big one in your stomach so that you can't bend in the middle any more.

The whole reason I was in that waiting room in the first place, in that predicament with a baby, a toddler and another baby, a pretty big one, taking up all that room under my ribs, kicking me in a not very friendly way all the time so that my ribs felt like I've been playing football with some very clumsy high school boys (not that I actually know any high school boys because I spend my time all the time with babies and toddlers and other pregnant ladies), was because of my husband.

Now, he's a pretty good husband, as husbands go, and I can't say that there's another one around that I would trade him for, since he picks up his own socks and eats whatever I cook for dinner and sometimes, not often, but sometimes rubs my back. But you can't deny, he's the reason I'm in this predicament. I told him I was tired and he said he couldn't sleep because he had this heartburn, so I told him to go take something for it and he said he had a better idea, and then he woke me up pretty good but not good enough for me to remember that I already had one baby and one toddler, and now here I am with this new baby, a pretty big one that seems to want to thrust a telescope out my belly button and there's still three weeks to go.

So I'm kind of sorry that he had that heartburn and maybe it's really all my fault because I didn't feel like cooking that day so I ordered pizza. And it wasn't even very good pizza.

A Stranger in a Lonely Place

TWO NIGHTS AGO, I WENT TO MASS. A memorial Mass for the people killed in the attack on the World Trade Center and the Pentagon. A thanksgiving Mass for all those who survived, and a Mass for peace and unity in the days to come.

I hated it.

The priest spoke of God and His love. How He was always there for us. How we can't lose our faith over acts that seem unbelievable, unexplainable, unforgivable. How God knows our grief and despair and will be holding our hands in the days ahead.

I didn't believe a word of it.

How could all this happen? How could God look down from His mighty throne and not stop those planes? How could He allow 20 madmen to kill over 6,000 people? Why would He? Have we turned away from Him too much? Are we so evil and despicable, in our greed for sensation and material things, for Him to reach out His hand and save us? People have spoken of 'miracles', of being within a hair's-breadth of being killed and yet somehow surviving. What does that mean for the ones that died? No one was willing to perform a miracle for them?

I'm angry. I'm so very angry. I want to scream and curse and hurl things across the room. I want to smack the face of every smug believer who says "these things happen for a reason, we can only have faith and pray". I want to beat the people who say "everything is going to be all right". I want to find the ones responsible and punish them until they wish they'd never lived. I want to...

I want to believe again. My God, it's lonely and scary here without You. Why have You forsaken us? Did You ever really exist? Did Mankind just dream You up, to help them through the terrifying unexplainable moments of life and death? Why do You allow these things? WHY?

It's been hard enough, even before September 11, to believe. I've been watching my mother die, watching her suffer, watching her wither and age and become frail in body and mind and tried to believe. Tried to tell myself there's a reason for everything, that God wouldn't make a good woman like her suffer for no reason. But damn it, God, You make it hard.

I still believe in people. The good they can do is overwhelming, and the kindness they can extend is what I always thought was Your body on earth. Your hands reaching out through them, Your words coming to me from their lips, Your love touching me through their acts of mercy. And now, I just don't know.

At the end of that Mass, I spoke with a friend. He said, "It's good to see everyone here, on their knees. I could feel God's love here." I told him I didn't. I didn't feel it there, in the church, and I didn't feel it here, in my heart. His eyes welled up and he hugged me, and I loved him for that. But I'm still scared and I'm lost in a lonely place.

God, help me believe. I feel like a stranger here now.

Rest Area, I-40

GOD'S RV BROKE DOWN OUTSIDE OF Asheville, heading west on I-40. I've heard the motors on those mini-Winnie's are just a little too small; at any rate, this one was popping and hissing. Not that it was any of my business. I just happened to stop at the same rest area, taking a bathroom break and hoping the drink machine carried some diet soda other than Pepsi. I don't know why you can never find a diet Sundrop or maybe a Fresca in the drink machines, but no, it's always the same damned diet cola.

The RV's hood had been raised and God just stood there, glancing into the engine and looking around to see if anyone would help. Oh, I knew it was God alright, although the ostrich-leather boots threw me off a bit. I've seen those kinds of boots, before but I never quite understood why anyone would wear them. Ostriches are some right ugly birds.

He saw me staring at them and smiled. "I believe everything has its use." Apparently that includes the skins of dead animals.

Jesus came out of the restroom, flapping his hands and wearing third-world chic. Loose-fitting trousers and tunic of some natural fiber, scraggly sandals made of felt, a toe ring. He grabbed a lawn chair and guitar out of the Winnie, sat down and began strumming. Jeez, I thought, he's bought into that whole Jesus Christ Superstar gig.

"Think you can help us out?" God asked. "Give us a lift?"

"Sorry," I said. "No can do."

It's not that I didn't feel sorry for them, stuck in a place like that and with the weather maybe going sour, but I didn't have room for them in my car. I could see the Virgin Mary, peering out through the windshield, a worried look on her face, and a little pang of guilt went through me, but when the Holy Spirit fluttered out of the Winnebago's side door as a dove and turned into Jim Carrey, well, I just couldn't do it. A person can only handle so much.

"You got a cell phone?" I asked. "Call the Highway Patrol. They'll help you out." I bought the damned diet Pepsi and a pack of Lance's Nip-Chee's and started to climb back into my van. It was a sure bet that a couple of tractor trailers or some tourists would be pulling into the rest area soon enough and somebody would give God a hand. This was the Bible-belt, after all.

"Oh come on. What are you afraid of? We just need a ride home."

"Well, can't you do it yourself? I mean, you know, the finger of God and all that? Just zap the sucker and it oughta start right up."

"Something tells me you're peeved," God chuckled. He had this deep throaty voice, and that laugh made him sound like all those other sure-they-know-everything Southern gentlemen I've been around all my life. Him with his boots and his crisply-ironed white shirt and crinkly laugh lines around his eyes. He made me sick.

"Look," I said, facing him and sticking my face in his. "I'm not all that interested, but tell you what - answer a few questions for me and I'll think about giving you a ride."

He nearly chuckled again, but I guess he saw the look on my face. "Okay," he said, spreading his hands, palms up. "Do I have a choice?"

Maybe it was a mistake, offering a deal like that, but how often do you get a chance to put God in the hot seat? Besides, I didn't think He'd really have any answers.

I admit to being a little distracted. The Holy Ghost kept slipping around; now here, now there, moving fast. A little flicker of light, a tongue of flame. Like something you see out of the corner of your eye, only when you turn to look at it, it's gone. Annoying as hell.

Mary didn't say a word. She came out of that RV with a basket and began setting up a picnic just as nice as you please. Long checkered cloth spread over one of the picnic tables. Paper plates and Solo cups. Now and then, she'd glance up at me and smile.

"So what are your questions?" God asked. "Something specific?" He settled himself on the bumper of the Winnebago, shoulders resting against the grille, hands on his knees. Light gleaming off the windshield behind him betrayed a secret truth – God was going bald.

I paced back and forth, hands in the pockets of my hoodie. "Okay, for starters, what about the Church? I was born in the Church, raised in it, but now I can't stand to go there. It's nothing but self-serving lies! After the September 11 attack, you know what our priest said? He said maybe it was Your way of getting people to return to the Church. Man, if death and destruction were the only way to get people to my house, I wouldn't be too proud about it. Maybe the time has come for a real shake-up, a new way of looking at religion. At faith in general."

"Don't confuse the two." God swung his foot up on his knee and loosely clasped his hands on it. "Faith is a belief. Religion is a system. And yes, I could agree that a shake-up is due."

"How will you bring that about?"

"I won't. It's not my job. That's Mankind's job."

"But it used to be your job. Back in the days of Noah and King David, you used to step in. Seems like lately you've been disassociating yourself. I haven't heard of a good bona fide involvement since you sent Jesus." Jesus snickered but didn't look up. He kept fingering the guitar, playing the opening notes to the acoustic version of 'Layla'. "I mean, *was* the September 11 attack meant to be a warning? Some kind of message about 'fly right or die'? It seems you leave an awful lot of stuff unclear."

God rubbed a hand over his face and sighed. "I tried. For a long time, I tried to make it real clear what the situation was. I created the world and I gave it to Mankind. Yes, maybe I micro-managed for a while, but I've grown up since then. Realized I can't run everything myself. It was pointless, anyway. Ever since I gave free will, nothing has turned out the way I expected. So I sent Jesus, trying to get the message through one last time. The kid did his best. As far as I'm concerned, I've done my job. Created the world. You think that was easy? You have no idea. The details, the headaches. Just try sometime, making something from nothing. Besides, it's supposed to be the Holy Spirit's job now, getting the Word out, but somehow I'm always the one who gets the flak."

I turned to look at the Holy Spirit, floating above us. "What do you say about that?" I asked him and he shrugged, disintegrating into wisps of smoke, and reorganizing near the trash bin as a Haitian refugee. His white teeth gleamed as he replied, "Honey, I work all the time, but God has the best PR. That's okay, I prefer anonymity. It's my stock-in-trade."

I turned back to God. "Your message – however you get it out – is pretty confusing. We're supposed to believe that you're all-powerful, yet you seem to do nothing about terrible wrongs. What about all the people killed in the earthquake in China? Was it really bad karma? What about the floods in the Midwest? The fires in California? Why let a tornado strike a Boy Scout Camp and let it slaughter four kids? Four *kids*, four *Boy Scouts*, for God's sake. Do you have it out for us or something? Do you WANT to wipe us out?" I could hear my voice scaling up, so I took a deep breath and asked again, more quietly, "Could you explain? An explanation would really be nice."

"There's a common misconception that I know what's going to happen. I don't." A frown creased God's face. "I'm like a great composer, or a painter. I create a masterpiece, but like any masterpiece it has a few flaws. Like earthquakes. Tectonic plates shift, pressure is released. I don't control what happens."

"Then why should we bother to pray to you? If you can't do anything, why should we follow your rules?" I flung my key ring down and threw out my hands. "See, this is what drives me crazy. You lay down the commandments. Keep holy the Sabbath day. Have no strange Gods. I mean, I 'get' the rest of them, no murders, no coveting, no stealing, but first and foremost, you order us to follow your way, and then you leave your way so god-damned confusing."

"Don't swear," Mary said softly. "I hate it when people swear. It hurts my ears." She opened a container of fried chicken. "Say 'gol-darned'. Or maybe use an adverb, like 'terribly'. Adverbs are nice."

God sighed again and rose to his feet. He's quite tall, a vigorous-looking man. I have to admit, he could be very attractive. He stuck his hands in his pockets, scuffed his boot up against the curb. "I've tried to make myself clear over the years. Believe me. But Mankind seems determined to misunderstand. To misinterpret. I even had Jesus explain that the most important thing was loving one another. But does anyone listen? The ten commandments were an effort to give guidelines. Jesus' sacrifice on the cross? More effort to give guidelines. There is no greater love, all that. And the Holy Spirit, trying to inspire love for each other in the hearts of Man, giving Mankind a conscience, an inner knowledge of right and wrong. What more do you want? Bumper stickers?" He sighed again and dropped down onto the picnic bench. "Besides, the Baptists do that already." He peered at me from beneath heavy eyebrows. "I sense that your anger is more specifically directed."

"Who says I'm angry?"

"Oh, please. I *invented* body language."

"Well, okay." I took a deep breath. "Okay. You really want to know why I'm angry? My mom. Was it necessary to do her like that?"

God folded his arms over his chest. Talk about body language, it was clear he didn't feel he should have to defend any decisions. "You think I treated her badly?"

"Yes! She's never hurt a single soul in her whole life, but you allowed her to have strokes, injuries, a broken hip, more strokes. You knocked her down again and again, like a cat toying with a mouse. If you were going to let her die all along, why bring her to the brink so many times, and allow her to live, while taking away all her abilities? Infection, pain, confusion. Unable to speak clearly, think clearly. It broke my heart! I can't love a God who treats my mother like that!"

"How would you want her to die? Cancer? Heart attack? Maybe she could get run over by a train. Everyone has to die."

"It's easy for you to talk!" I turned to Jesus. "After all, God allowed your mother to rise bodily to Heaven. How would you have felt if God had made her suffer?"

Jesus raised his eyes to me. Deep brown, almost black. For a moment, his fingers stilled on the guitar

278

strings. "She suffered. Didn't you, Ma?" We both glanced over at Mary. She nodded but didn't look at us, just pressed her lips tightly together, folding paper napkins. Again, to me, Jesus said, "She suffered. When I died. At least your mother didn't have to do that, didn't have to watch her children die. All her children are still alive."

"Look, I understand about suffering . . ."

"Do you?" God's voice boomed and I jumped. "What – exactly – do you understand?"

"Well, you know, that we are all doomed to suffer. It's part of being human. I mean, I expect to suffer, it's just. . ." My stammering wound down under the wilting glare of his eyes. With one last effort, I burst out, "But I couldn't stand watching my mother suffer!"

"So it's really all about you. *Your* pain, watching her." God closed his eyes.

"It's NOT about me! It was my mother's situation that – "

"And what was so terrible about it? She died warm, dry, and resting in bed. Not in the mud. Not seeing her children slaughtered. You think her way of going is so horrible? Most of it's due to the medical industry anyway. They're the ones who've built fortunes keeping people alive past their 'sell-by' date. Why is everyone so afraid of death? Haven't I made it clear by now that it's not how you die that matters? It's how you live!"

279

Mary finished setting the table and closed the picnic basket. "You two need to calm down. How about a nice glass of wine?" She pulled out a bottle of chardonnay. To me, she added, "He shouldn't give you such a hard time. You're a good girl. I saw you, taking care of your mother. You wore yourself out. He really could have made it easier." She shot God a reproving glance before handing round the pickles.

My hands were trembling as I sat down and spread a napkin over my lap. I wasn't going to cry. Not before God. "Mom had such a great day, that last day before she fell. She was so happy. Who'd have ever thought she'd find love again at her age? You brought Edward into her life, gave her a glimpse of joy, then you let her fall and break her hip and it was downhill ever after. Why'd you have to lift her up, only to slam her down?"

There was silence for a moment. The Holy Spirit, now a curly-haired miniature poodle, trotted over to the bench and jumped on God's lap. He smiled at me - the Holy Spirit, that is - his pink tongue showing between doggy teeth. "Who's your daddy?" he smirked.

"Oh shut up," I said. "You think you're so funny."

God continued his silence, scratching the Holy Spirit absent-mindedly behind the ear. Finally, God said, "Look. I gave you life. I *gave* it to you, to all Mankind. I gave you a world in which to live. What you do with it is up to you. I don't control your life. I don't have a 'plan' for it. People like to believe I do, but that's wishful thinking. It's more like I have a *wish* for your life. That you find it within yourself to be useful, to do things for others, to become bigger than just one person by reaching out to other people, by giving of your self. That's all. Pretty simple, at least I've always thought so. And then, when your life is over, *whenever* it's over, *however* it's over, I bring you home. I don't *kill* you. Disease might kill you, or the events of Man, or a natural disaster, but all I do is bring you home, to Heaven."

"But couldn't you make it easier? Not allow so much suffering? Why did my mother have to go through – "

"You're really stuck on that, aren't you? Like a skip in an old 45 rpm record. It's that one thing that really soured you on me. You've focused on that and lost all sense of perspective."

His tone was accusing and I found myself on the defensive. "Well, the very first words you said to me was that you believe in usefulness. I don't *get it*. What's useful about my mom having stroke after stroke, losing her abilities, losing her intelligence? What's useful about children suffering from the acts of pedophiles, or people born with terrible handicaps? What's useful about 150,000 people losing their lives in a tsunami? And don't give me that crap about how maybe they're born to teach others about compassion! Why make one individual suffer to teach another a lesson? That's so stupid!"

"Is it? Well, golly gosh, I guess I blew it then with Christ's passion!" God brushed the Holy Spirit off his lap and leaned forward again. He started to reach for my hand, but I drew back. The Holy Spirit turned into the crazy lady who wears scripture sandwich boards at the corner of Independence Boulevard and Fourth Street and winked at me. "Besides, that's not what I'm doing," God said, his voice gentle. "You don't understand. Your mother was loved. She was loved, so much, by you and your brother and sisters. She was *loved*. No matter how many 'bad' things happened to her, she was still more fortunate than most. *And she knew how much you love her.* Think about it – if she'd died peacefully in her sleep, eleven years ago, before her first stroke – would she have known? Would you? Would you trade the good moments of the past eleven years? The times you were able to admire her strength? To respect her feelings? To bathe her, dress her, feed her, to care lovingly for her as you would a child? I gave you life so you could do those things. That's what life is *for*."

"But it was so painful to lose her. I couldn't - " The words stopped, without volition, and my mouth filled with tears.

"This is not about you. Remember?" God paused, then softly touched my hair. "I know it's hard. That why I wish you'd lean on me a bit. I felt so bad when you lost your faith. If only you could believe. She really was blessed. She had her family."

"She deserved more. We weren't enough."

"Yes, you were. *I* think you were."

The Holy Spirit, in the form of my next-door neighbor, sat close to me and took my hand. Mary handed a loaf of bread to Jesus and he tore a hunk off, dipped it in the wine, and offered it to me. I closed my eyes, fighting the feeling, refusing to give in. The anger had sustained me for such a long time.

"I suppose you're going to tell me she's in a better place," I said, looking at God.

"She is. Heaven's great! I've tried to give previews of coming attractions – sunrises, butterflies, rainy days."

"Rainy days?"

"Yes." He smiled, a relaxed happy grin. "I love the rain. Evaporation and condensation were two of my best ideas."

Jesus nodded and added, "Music, too. Don't forget music." The Holy Spirit turned into Gene Kelly and danced around, crooning 'I'm Singing in the Rain, Just Singing in the Rain'. Everyone laughed. Well, except me.

"I don't know, God," I said, trying to regain my composure. "It sure seems like you could have arranged things better. Kept the confusion down. If I could have

283

just believed there was a reasonable point to all this . . ."

"Yes," he said. "If you could have just believed. But that's okay. I'd say I forgive you, but you'd probably think I was being condescending. Let's just say, I understand. Are we friends again?"

I wasn't sure. I wanted to believe it was a simple as that. But lost faith isn't like lost car keys. Sometimes, when it's gone, it's pure gone. "How do I know you're not just my imagination? Something to hold onto when there's nothing else? Maybe Mankind invented you because otherwise the world's too scary."

"Then who invented Mankind?" God finished his wine and touched the napkin to his lips. "Look, I can deal with your doubts. After all, I don't always understand you, either. Ever think about that? You're much too apt to be a quitter. To lose faith, not only in me, but in yourself. Why is that?"

"Well," I reminded him, "I *am* fallible. You made me that way."

"No excuse."

I had to admit that he'd answered my questions. Of course, the answers raised more questions, but in all fairness, he'd been a pretty good egg about it and deserved his ride home. As we packed up the picnic stuff, he said, "Listen, for what it's worth - I know I've made mistakes. Plenty of them. But don't discount the outpouring of help that people give when something goes wrong. Sometimes it takes a disaster before my children discover the great depths of compassion they carry. *That's* what I planted in humanity. The ability to care. You don't see it anywhere else. Not in the plants or rocks or clouds, but in Mankind. Oh, maybe a few of the higher animal orders. I was practicing there. I didn't put that ability into you for no reason at all."

"Yes, people care! But they still go to war, too. You also gave us the ability to fight and compete and cheat and lie…"

"That's right. You have abilities and you have choices!" God's shoulders slumped and he turned away, gathering trash and throwing it in the bin. "Well, if you don't need anything from me, I'll be going."

He told Jesus to get in the Winnebago and give the engine a crank. It started up first try. I guess he didn't need a ride after all. The Holy Spirit turned into a chickadee and flew away, while Mary gave me a hug and a Ziploc full of brownies. "Take care," she whispered. "I'll say hi to your Mom for you."

I cleared my throat and shuffled my feet, trying to think of a final weighty comment to make to God, but my mind was blank. He was different from what I'd expected. I'd felt so abandoned. It wasn't possible to let those feelings go all at once. He waited patiently, leaning against the door frame, offering sympathy I didn't want. Seems like lately, whenever someone's

285

nice to me, I start to cry. "Well, drive safely," I began, knowing it was a lame comment.

"You too."

Again, an awkward pause. Something was missing. Some final note on which a new relationship could begin. Maybe. "I'll think about what you said."

"Don't think too much. Just *feel*." His gaze slid away from mine for a moment and I saw great sorrow on His face. Then he shook it off and gave me a stern look. "Call me. Anytime. You've got my number."

"Why? So you can remind me that you can't do anything about anything?"

"No. So I can remind you that you CAN."

"What are we to you?" I whispered. "An experiment? Are we just your toys, like a child plays with dolls? Do we exist merely to gratify your ego?"

"You are my children," he said. "And I love you."

He patted my shoulder, climbed up into his rig and said good-bye. I watched the Winnebago drive slowly out of the rest area and I wondered where He was going. Guess I'll never know.

Still unsure, I got into my van and started the engine. Put in a CD of YoYoMa playing Bach's prelude. Yeah, the music was beautiful, and so were the mountains and the sun shining down. Was God responsible for all of that? I don't know. How much of life is random happenings, chance, the lucky jackpot for some while others crap out? When people do good things, is it because God inspired them or do they deserve the credit themselves? And maybe none of the answers to these questions really matter in the end, because when you come right down to it, believe in God or not, it IS how you live that matters. It's all you have.

I pulled out onto the freeway ramp, traveling on. Ol' YoYo swung into an Aaron Copeland number, kinda jazzy, and I popped open the can of diet Pepsi. Took a swig, and nearly passed out, held the damned can up before my unbeliever's eyes. Wouldn't you just know?

Fresca.

Appendix

After the Wink was previously published online at *HotRead.com, Conversely.com, eastoftheweb.com*, and *alt.write.com*, and in print in *Sexy Shorts, Speak Up Italy, Speak Up Spain, TBRA Publishing,* and *Mind the Gap*. It was made into a short student film by Jonathon Martofel, and broadcast on radio by Evergreen Radio Reading Service for the *5th Saturday* program, KUOW, Seattle.

Jim was previously published online at *BoomerWomenSpeak.com*

Me and Mom and the Very Bad Day was previously published in *Caregivers Magazine*.

Just Hear Those Sleighbells Jing-a-ling, Oh Natalie!, and Frozen in Place were previously published together online at *Eclectica.org* along with three stories by David Bulley. We competed with each other and produced these six stories in six days. One of the best writing challenges I ever experienced.

Coming to My Senses was a prizewinner in the BBC *"dotdotdot…"* competition and dramatized for broadcast on BBC-4. It was also previously published online at *Eclectica.org*, and made into a short film by Chad Richards of *thefilmcommune.*

…in Love & War was previously published online at *Eclectica.org*.

Cubby Holes was previously published in *Skirt! Magazine*.

Don't Let Me Bother You was previously published in *Lonzie's Fried Chicken*.

Say It was previously published online at *LiteraryPotpourri.com*, and in print in *Ink Pot* and *TBRA Publishing.*

Room 506, Bed 2 was displayed with other poetry at the opening ceremony for the NC Women's Hospital, Chapel Hill.

Another Weekend with Susie was the first short story I ever wrote. It was a prizewinner in the 1998 Elizabeth Simpson Smith short story competition at the Charlotte Writers Club, previously published online at *Eclectica.org* and also published in their first anthology, and a prizewinner in *Peninsular* magazine, UK.

Water's Edge was previously published in *Lonzie's Fried Chicken*, online at *Espresso Fiction*, and in the Charlotte Writers Club 2007 anthology, *Only Connect*.

Seven Warning Signs that will Save Your Life was previously published online in *APT* magazine.

Something to Talk About was previously published in the Charlotte Writers Club 2005 anthology.

The Warm Curve of the Throat was previously published in *City Primeval*, and online at *Eclectica.org* (the featured story that month).

Oral Tradition: *Fussing in the Key of G* was previously published online by *Espresso Fiction* and *eastoftheweb.com*, and in the Cambridge University Press anthology, *Happy Families?*

Flags Waving was previously published online at *eastoftheweb.com*.

But Who's Counting? was my first published short story, in *Independence Boulevard*. Thanks, M. Scott Douglas.

The Last Noel was previously published in *BuzzWords*, UK.

Going to Vermont was previously published in *Skirt! Magazine* and *BuzzWords*, UK.

Oh! the Overnight was previously published in *BuzzWords,* UK.

Then the Sharks was previously published online at *memoriesofwar.com* and broadcast on radio by Evergreen Radio Reading Service for the *5ᵗʰ Saturday* program, KUOW, Seattle.

The Last Time Dad Got Out of Jail was previously published online at *Eclectica.org*.

Litter Box Full was previously published online at *LiteraryPotpourri.com* and in print in *Ink Pot*.

Cello, Standard was previously published online at *NewVietArt.net*

No Anchovies was published in *Short Stuff Magazine* and *The Eclectic Reader*, and online at *HotRead.com*.

A Stranger in a Lonely Land was previously published online at *InPosseReview,* a literary journal at *Webdelsol.com*

Rest Area, I-40 was previously published in the Charlotte Writers' Club Anthology of November 2008, *Journey Without*.

Acknowledgements

The stories in this collection were written between 1999 and 2008, and reflect my growth and change as a writer. I consider myself fortunate to have found some many willing publishers and encouraging editors for my short fiction, particularly the online e-zines which generally operated without funds and strictly through the love of literature by their editors. I am particularly indebted to *eastoftheweb,* Tom Dooley of *Eclectica,* Zoe King of *BuzzWords* and Beverly Jackson of *Literary Potpourri,* for being willing to publish my work a number of times.

During the years I wrote these stories, I received considerable support from various writers' website, including *writers-bbs.com, stwa.net,* and a couple of no-longer-existing writers' message boards, such as Author!Author! and Lifeboat. I also was a member of Alex Keegan's Boot Camp, and survived the lash and scourge to become a better writer. Thanks, Alex! Also thanks to some of the people who really encouraged me at these websites. 'Ta' to John Ravenscroft, Chris Jevi, Brent Olson, the late Glenn Osborn, Yasemine Galenorn (NY Times bestselling author!), F. John

Sharp, Kathleen McCall, Zoe King, Rusty Barnes, Timothy Gager, Virginia Lee, David Bulley, David King, Elizabeth Ann Roy, GiGi Dane, Gregory Banks, Lois Peterson, Maire O'Reilly, Mare Freed, Maryanne Stahl, Terry Proffer, Tomi Rae, Wendy Ogden, and "Bwana". I've loved hanging out with y'all.

Thanks to Ben Plunkett who helped me design the front cover.

As always, thanks to my family, and especially my husband Matt, who has been nagging me to get this collection together. I hope you enjoy it.

Books by Carolyn Steele Agosta

Every Little Step She Takes
The Pleasure of Your Company
After the Wink and other stories

Visit my website at http://www.carolynagosta.com